D0391764

What the critics are saying about...

Against The Wall

"WHOA!!! AGAINST THE WALL is off the chart in heat! Ryan and Shea ignite the pages from page one...Find out what happens, who gets whom up AGAINST THE WALL in this hot, startlingly steamy tale." - *Ansley Velarde, The Road to Romance*

"...Ms. Byrd's story of two lovers finding their way into each other's heart is an entertaining read. While reading this, be prepared to squirm in your seat." – *Thia McClain, The Romance Reader's Connection*

"Against the Wall is a really good book, one that I couldn't put down...The sex is beyond hot and the couple burn up the pages both in and out of bed. Rhyannon Byrd has done an excellent job writing this story of love that won't be denied." – *Angel Brewer, Just Erotic Romance Reviews*

Waiting For It

5 Roses! "If you enjoy highly erotic contemporary stories, with a heavy dose of emotion thrown in and a beautiful HEA (happily ever after) ending to top it off, give Waiting for It a try." - *Mireya, A Romance Review*

Recommended Read at RTR! "Explosive sex, heart-wrenching emotions...as well as two characters that are unforgettable, make this a must read." - *Tracey West, The Road to Romance*

5 Stars! "Jake is one of the few heroes I've seen who could be incredibly sweet and vulnerable...yet still be totally Alpha. ...one book everyone should read!" - *Dani Jacquel, Just Erotic Romance Reviews*

Magick Men: A Shot of Magick

"Magick Men: A Shot of Magick was definitely a book worth reading. A short story, it still had all the elements of a longer story...Truly a good short story, I can't wait for the rest of the series!" – *Julia, The Romance Studio*

"...truly a fantastic and captivatingly romantic story. I could not put this book down. I hope that Ms. Byrd will write the sequel and give us the story of the next warlock in line to find his soul mate. Magick Men: A Shot of Magick is an erotically stimulating read." - *Dianne Nogueras, eCataRomance Reviews*

"...If you like your hero super alpha with attitude, sarcasm, and a sexy as hell growl, you will definitely find him right here. The only disappointing thing is that it wasn't longer. For a good quick read I strongly recommend Magick Men: A Shot of Magick. You won't be sorry, trust me." – *Faith Jacobs, Just Erotic Romance Reviews*

AGAINST THE WALL

Rhyannon Byrd

AGAINST THE WALL
An Ellora's Cave Publication, December 2004

Ellora's Cave Publishing, Inc.
PO Box 787
Hudson, OH 44236-0787

ISBN #1419951114

Other available formats: Microsoft Reader (LIT), Adobe (PDF),
Rocketbook (RB), Mobipocket (PRC) & HTML

Copyright © 2004 Rhyannon Byrd

ALL RIGHTS RESERVED. This book may not be reproduced in
whole or in part without permission.

This book is a work of fiction and any resemblance to persons,
living or dead, or places, events or locales is purely coincidental.
They are productions of the authors' imagination and used
fictitiously.

Edited by *Pamela Campbell*
Cover art by *Syneca*

Warning:

The following material contains graphic sexual content meant for mature readers. *Against The Wall* has been rated E–rotic by a minimum of three independent reviewers.

Ellora's Cave Publishing offers three levels of Romantica™ reading entertainment: S (S-ensuous), E (E-rotic), and X (X-treme).

S-*ensuous* love scenes are explicit and leave nothing to the imagination.

E-*rotic* love scenes are explicit, leave nothing to the imagination, and are high in volume per the overall word count. In addition, some E-rated titles might contain fantasy material that some readers find objectionable, such as bondage, submission, same sex encounters, forced seductions, etc. E-rated titles are the most graphic titles we carry; it is common, for instance, for an author to use words such as "fucking", "cock", "pussy", etc., within their work of literature.

X-*treme* titles differ from E-rated titles only in plot premise and storyline execution. Unlike E-rated titles, stories designated with the letter X tend to contain controversial subject matter not for the faint of heart.

AGAINST THE WALL

Rhyannon Byrd

Prologue

The first words to pop into her head were strange ones—a resurrection from the warmth of childhood in an instinctual attempt to find comfort in the decidedly uncomfortable.

I don't think we're in Kansas anymore...

How wonderfully mad to be quoting *The Wizard of Oz*, she mused—but standing in the doorway of Red's Bar, Shea Dresden felt a strange affinity with the displaced Dorothy and her little dog. Red's was definitely a far cry from her usual haunts. Places like the university's lecture hall and library.

Yeah, okay, so she was a geek. No one knew that better than she. But she was a determined geek, damn it, and no Wicked Witch of the West or burly looking bully was going to send her running before she got what she'd come here for!

Yeah, you go girl, her woman's pride cheered, and Shea put everything she had into focusing on the rallying war cry, rather than the flurry of nervous energy pumping through her overexcited system. Her body quaked with it, and the smoke-filled air only made the nauseating exhilaration that much worse.

It wasn't that she couldn't stand a little smoke. Heck, she smoked sometimes herself, when she got too restless or tense—or just needed an excuse to sit on her balcony listening for her next-door neighbor Ryan. But this wasn't just a little smoke. The inside of Red's was dingy gray with the thickness of it, and Shea knew when she left she'd still be able to smell it on her clothes and in her hair.

Not that I'm wearing all that many clothes, she thought with a wry twist of her lips, but then she was here to meet a man.

And not just any man, honey, her incessantly complaining libido chimed in, *but Ryan McCall, the sexiest damn thing we've ever set eyes on!*

Ryan was everything Shea thought a man should be, and gorgeous to boot. Tall, tawny-headed, and ruggedly, insanely, *made you want to wrestle him to the nearest bed* handsome.

Without a doubt, the quintessential stud.

Shea wanted him unlike anything she'd ever wanted before. Wanted him enough to swallow her stupid pride and do whatever—*whatever*—it took to get him. She was done accepting his casual brush-offs. Done tiptoeing around that infuriating distance he insisted on maintaining between them.

Tonight, she was ready to get as up close and personal as two people could get. Ready to slip under his guard and batter down his defenses until she'd gotten as far into him as he'd worked his way into her. She wanted it all, every single intoxicating detail that made him so irresistible. Wanted absolute access to every breathtaking inch of skin, muscle, and bone. Wanted to know firsthand how it felt to be at the mercy of all that overwhelmingly raw, masculine power.

That's why she was here.

"When he wants a woman," her best friend Hannah had told her, "Ry likes to hang out at Red's. It's not that it's really dangerous or anything, but it definitely caters to a rough and tumble kind of crowd. Let's just say it's not the kind of place where you and I would hang out, but Ry does just fine there."

Shea had wanted to know why someone as gorgeous as Ryan McCall didn't have a steady girlfriend, when he could so obviously have his choice of any woman he wanted.

And that had been Hannah's answer.

Red Mackey's Bar.

Ryan, it seemed, preferred a no-strings-attached brand of sex—and he found it at Red's.

It was hard to believe the sexy ATF agent resorted to this place for his pleasure, but Hannah had known Ryan forever. If she said he went to Red's to get laid, then Shea knew it was true. Why he would come here to look for a woman was beyond her, but here she was, ready to do her best to finally get the stud right where she wanted him.

Sure, she didn't know a whole heck of a lot about playing the part of a hot, willing, available woman, but no way in hell was she letting that hold her back. Tonight, Shea intended to be that woman—the one—*the woman*, which was why her palms were damp and her stomach was flip-flopping with sexual tension, winding her up tight enough to snap.

It wasn't that she was afraid. Not of Ryan—not of how she felt about him—and she sure as hell wasn't afraid of what she wanted from him.

The only thing she feared now was failure—but tonight, it wasn't going to be an option.

She worried about going through life never craving another human being the way she craved him. But she had it now, that heady, beautiful burn of need spearing through her system, and all she wanted to do was embrace it. Celebrate it. Satisfy it. She wanted to surrender and succumb to it, drowning her senses…drenching them in the ravenous, insatiable, consuming feelings of heart-pounding lust and sexual hunger that this man inspired in her. Wanted to fill up on the dizzying rush of energy that just looking at him pumped through her veins, filling her cells, until she felt packed full of life.

And more than anything in the world, she wanted to be packed full of that beautiful bad boy.

All she had to do was find him. Of course, beneath the eerie, flickering glow of the fluorescent beer signs, that was probably going to be harder than she'd expected.

Damn, and here she'd thought this would be the easy part. It was Friday night, and despite its nitty-gritty interior, Red's was packed with people. Men and women obviously looking for a place where they could drown their sorrows and hook up with a warm body for the night.

And Shea knew Ryan wasn't much of a drinker.

She also knew he wasn't much on relationships either, but she hoped to change that. At least that was the plan. The first part of the plan, though, was to get sex. Lots and lots of hard, heavy, mind-shattering sex — with Ryan.

From the look of the women strutting around, Shea didn't need to use her Ph.D. to get a fairly good idea of what drew him here week after week. Yep, Hannah had definitely been right on that score. The nervous, excited, kind of sick feeling in her stomach twisted into something sharper — something green and possessive that made her want to corner every woman in the place and demand the nature of their association with *her* man.

When a heavy-chested redhead with legs that looked longer than Shea's entire body strolled by, drinks balanced perfectly on a tray in her manicured hand, Shea had the compelling urge to start with her. The redhead looked like just the type of woman she imagined Ryan using for a hard ride to take the edge off. She had the most ridiculous impulse to go and stomp on the woman's red-painted toes. Too bad she knew she'd never really do such a thing, because thinking of the sexy bar server and Ryan together made the idea sweetly satisfying.

It hit her out of the blue, the overwhelming enormity of what she was trying to accomplish here. The knowledge of what was at stake stormed through her body, leaving an uncomfortable prickling sensation in its wake. Suddenly, she felt incredibly stupid standing there in her new J. Crew summer dress. It was slinky black silk, bought especially for the occasion, along with the matching high-heeled sandals that were slowly killing her poor feet. She'd even left her glossy black curls free to spiral around her face in a style the women's magazines had said would look both womanly and flirtatious.

Like Dorothy slipping into her ruby slippers, Shea had felt transported to another world as she donned the weapons of her seduction, piece by sensual piece, down to the tiny black thong hidden beneath her dress. She didn't so much wonder if she *could* do this, as feel that she *had* to do this. It was serendipity. Everything in the universe had come together at this specific moment in time to give her this one shot — this one cosmically designed chance to take what she wanted.

And what she wanted was her gorgeous neighbor.

When she'd cast that last glance in the mirror before leaving her apartment, she'd actually thought she stood a chance of attracting Ryan's attention tonight. Without a doubt, she looked better…sexier than ever before, but now she no longer felt quite so confident.

She'd wanted Ryan to see her as something other than his brainy next-door neighbor—wanted him to see there was so much more to the black-haired little mouse with firm, somewhat smallish breasts and nonexistent hips who he seemed to regard as a quirky nuisance every time she sought him out.

But maybe it wasn't going to work.

Next to the hourglass figures in Red's, Shea figured she looked more average than ever. She didn't even want to think about the sexy redhead, whose figure was the kind Shea had always dreamed of but never developed. When compared to a woman like her—well, she knew it'd be a miracle if he even noticed she had her own set of breasts.

Hey, these babies are just fine, her pride muttered, clearly losing patience with her for faltering, and not getting a move on. *They're cute and perky, and you know the old saying, honey, "Anything more than a handful and you're risking a tongue sprain!"*

She's right, her cheeky libido echoed, *and we want that tongue in prime condition! Have I ever told you girls about that last fantasy I had? The one where he throws me on the bed and shoves that wicked tongue of his straight up my —*

Enough, Shea laughed over the sultry feminine voices in her mind, hoping like hell she wasn't going to need psychiatric help anytime soon. Never would be even better, but she wasn't holding out much hope at this point.

Or did all women have these strange little conversations in their heads?

Of course they do, drawled her asinine voice of reason. *Why else would men find us so difficult to comprehend?*

Because they're always thinking with their little head instead of their big one, smirked her pride, and Shea almost choked on another sudden burst of amusement.

Mmm, I don't know about that, her libido clucked mischievously. *From the look of Ryan's package, I'd say he's got a positively huge, um, brain hidden down in those pants of his. More than enough to do any "thinking" that needs to be done, though I'll be happy to give him any suggestions, should the magnificent stud req —*

Cut it out, Shea groaned, biting her tongue to keep from giggling out loud. Her moment of panic had passed, and she was back in action mode, her feminine wiles having effectively done their job and boosted her resolve.

So she didn't have boobs that spilled out of her neckline.

So what?

Maybe her sex appeal was more subtle than Red's regulars, maybe her looks didn't scream *Hey buddy, fuck me blind!*, but she was going to be damned before she let it stop her tonight. She'd come here to get laid by the only man she'd ever really wanted sinking between her legs, and by God, she wasn't leaving until she got him!

"But where the hell is he?" she mumbled beneath her breath, squinting into the dim interior while trying to locate Ryan in the shadowed booths and corners. She wasn't budging until she found him, and from the look of things, she might be using the pepper spray she'd stuffed in her black-beaded handbag long before she did.

The place could've given the term "meat market" its name. If the women looked easy, then the men looked like an advertisement for why good girls should stay home at night and let the party girls have all the fun. But screw it. Shea was tired of being good, and there was only one man she wanted to get down and dirty with and that was Ryan.

And if anything, she'd learned enough from the Jimmy debacle to trust her instincts...and hold out for what she really wanted.

Having made it this far, she at least had to find Ryan—had to hope there might be even the smallest chance he'd finally see her as that single, available, very *willing* woman he was looking for. If he took the bait, she was going to let him do anything he wanted to her, so long as she got a chance to do it all right back.

And although she might lack a lot of hands-on experience, her imagination worked just fine. The decadent thought of having his long, golden body laid out like a feast for her pleasure, his magnificent cock hers to do with as she pleased, had been her private fantasy for weeks now.

But it was time for the fantasy to end.

It was time for her to put her all into it and make a reality of the fact that she wanted to be taken long and hard and deep—*and not just for a one-night stand.*

Uh-uh. No way. Once she got him, she planned on keeping him.

But there was no need to blurt her intentions right out and scare the blasted man away forever. If the idea of having coffee with her turned him pale, she was pretty sure the idea of commitment would send him running scared. So her plan was really quite simple. As soon as she got his cooperation, she was going to take him to bed and give him everything—her body, heart, and soul—and show him just how much she loved him by giving him the best damn fuck of his life.

These women strutting around with their wealth of sexual expertise might have it on her when it came to time in the field, but none of them could top the fact that when Ryan was breaking her open, filling her up, he was going to be piercing a hell of a lot more than her body—and driving straight to her heart.

She only hoped tonight worked, because this was the last of her and Hannah's brilliant schemes. Who knew what she'd have to resort to if he turned her down tonight? She'd spent the last three months flirting and smiling with the gorgeous jerk, only to come up empty-handed time and again.

Heck, she'd even worked up the nerve to ask him out a few times, but something always kept him from accepting her awkwardly worded invitations. So this was it. The coup de grâce, and she wasn't stopping until she got him right where she wanted him, which was buried so deep inside of her that he could satisfy this aching emptiness once and for all.

Okay, so far, so good, she thought with a little smile, the exhilaration of the chase settling between her legs with a warm rush of anticipation. This was going to be so damn sweet.

Then again, she silently stuttered over a sudden lurch of panic as a big, sandy-haired bruiser caught sight of her and began heading her way, maybe this plan wasn't so damn hot after all.

Maybe she should've brought Hannah.

Or an army.

Or maybe she should just get the hell outta there!

Shea tried to conceal her alarm, praying the guy would leave her alone so she could get on with her hunt, but she didn't think she was going to be so lucky. Hannah had warned her that this place could sometimes get rowdy—hence the pepper spray—but she hadn't let herself fret over the fact that she just might have to use it. Like an idiot, she'd envisioned walking in, spotting Ryan, and getting the two of them out of there as fast as possible. Now she was going to have to open her purse, grab the spray, and pray she had better aim than sense.

Oh, hell, it was too late!

"Whadisa purty lil' piece like you doin' here?" the guy slurred in her face, his words and look clearly speaking of too much alcohol and too little cognitive brain power. His sour breath nearly made her go cross-eyed. *Ugh!* His bloodshot eyes stared straight at her quivering chest, and Shea felt an uncomfortable fear begin to form, strongly and rapidly, within her shivering limbs. It sat in the back of her throat, making her gag. Or maybe that was just the man's noxious odor, like sweat and smoke and sour whiskey all rolled into one.

Oh Jesus, what have I gotten myself into now? No one in this place was going to get in this creep's way, and Ryan appeared to be nowhere in sight. After all her preparation and determination not to be intimidated in this place, it was mortifying to feel the small cry begin to work its way up through her tight throat as the jerk's clammy hand wrapped around her upper arm, hurting her with bruising force. Pepper spray, a kick to his nuts, scratching his eyes out—crap, the opportunities were endless, but she just stood there like a trapped little rabbit.

Come on, you idiot, snap out of it!

She tried to listen to her outraged pride, but she could feel the scream coming—up, up, up—clawing at the back of her throat, and then salvation came from the last place she'd ever expected to find it.

"Leave her alone, Rich," the pretty redhead ordered, wedging her well-curved body between them. "I mean it," she warned in a hard voice. "One more mess-up from you and Red'll not only kick you out for good, but I'll tell McCall, and he'd be more than happy to deal with your sorry ass."

The look coming from Rich's bleary-eyed glare burned into the other woman, but she held her ground, calling his bluff, or maybe just crazy enough to be unafraid of him. Shea didn't care which, as long as he let her go so she could regroup. With a malicious sneer, he slowly released his painful grip on her arm. She barely resisted the urge to rub the dull sting away, finding just enough stubborn pride to keep from giving the big jerk the satisfaction of knowing he'd hurt her.

Instead, Shea held her breath and waited until he finally turned around, watching him stumble back over to the bar. The rickety wooden stool groaned in protest beneath his beefy weight as he motioned the bartender over for another refill, then hunched back over his choice of poison like a wild animal protecting its kill.

She watched him for a moment more and then, when she was sure he'd forgotten about her, she ran her fingers through her curls, straightened her dress, and took three deep, smoke-filled breaths. The mundane tasks were all part of a mental pep talk to get her back in the swing of things. She needed to get it together, because drunken assholes were going to be the least of her troubles tonight.

No, she still had one major problem—one big, outrageously handsome, entirely *too-sexy-for-her-own-good* kind of problem. Ryan. Despite the fact that she'd smiled and gazed with undisguised longing into his mesmerizing blue eyes more times than she could count, the man remained completely oblivious to her need for him. Other men had taken note of the change in her, the awakening physical hunger, and reacted to it like a pack of dogs following the scent of sex—just never the man she wanted.

It was annoying as hell, but Shea knew she shouldn't be all that surprised. After all, she was hoping to change the inexperienced part, but there wasn't anything she could do about being a sexually repressed, brainy introvert; at least not without the stud's cooperation.

She'd wasted months lusting from afar, but all of that was about to change. At least that was her hope before she heard, "I'd get on outta here if I were you."

Well, hell.

"Come on, honey, you gotta go," the woman drawled out the side of her candy-apple-red mouth. "He's a mean enough bastard when he's sober, but once he hits the bottle he becomes downright stupid. I want you gone before he causes anymore trouble and Red fires my ass."

This woman had just saved her from God only knew what, and Shea couldn't help but feel guilty for the way she'd been thinking about her and her toes when she'd first arrived. She wanted to argue and dig her heels into the sawdust-covered floor, unable to believe she was being kicked out of this hellhole while the drunken jerk-off got to stay, but she didn't want the woman losing her job because of her. Even if the lady was one of Ryan's women, she'd gone out of her way to look out for her when no one else would have. Though she hated the hell out of it, Shea couldn't help but give into the begrudging gratitude that allowed her to let the woman steer her back out the bar's entrance.

As they walked through the swinging wooden doors, the redhead looked Shea up and down with obvious curiosity. Once they were outside in the frigid night air, she lit up a Marlboro Red and rasped, "Just what were you doing in there?"

Well, gee, what do you think?

"I was, ah, looking for a friend of mine. Ryan McCall."

Two red eyebrows raised in surprise. "Ry? No shit. Man, he really is gonna be pissed when he hears about Rich."

Shea wrapped her arms around herself, trying to hold in her bitter disappointment, and burning streak of jealousy. "So you know Ryan personally, huh?"

The other woman smiled, clearly understanding the train of Shea's thoughts. "Yeah, I know him, but not like you're thinking, honey. Though God knows I'd change that sad fact if I could. Any woman in her right mind would. Now you go on and get outta here. Ryan's not here tonight and Red'll kill me if Rich causes anymore trouble."

"Well, um, thanks for what you did," Shea said softly, feeling immeasurably better that the redhead, whose name she still didn't know, wasn't intimately involved with Ryan—and frustrated beyond belief that apparently she wasn't going to be either. At least not tonight. The perfect friggin' chance and she'd crashed and burned before she even found him.

"Serendipity my ass," she grumbled, climbing into her silver Jetta. With a hollow feeling in the pit of her stomach, she slipped off her killer sandals and tossed them in the passenger's seat. Then she pulled out a stale pack of cigarettes from her glove compartment, lit one up and took a long drag, choking on a bitter combination of smoke and disappointment. She took a few more drags, crunched the rest out in her spotless ashtray, and finally drove home without ever looking back.

Chapter One

ATF Agent Ryan McCall and his longtime pal, Detective Derek Kiely, were all but dead on their feet as they dragged their tall, aching bodies through the front door of Ryan's Dunwoody apartment. Derek slumped down on the dark sofa while Ryan made his way into the small kitchen to fix them both ice packs for their throbbing faces.

They'd spent the evening on a joint sting operation, busting a local gun dealer who'd been selling weapons to gang kids on the side. A couple of the criminal's young security punks had made a run for it, and it'd been Ryan and Derek who chased down the gruesome duo. The street kids had fought to the ragged end, and the two "old dudes" were now feeling the pain.

Ryan took out two plastic bags, filled them with crushed ice, then walked back into his living room and tossed one over to Derek. "Damn," he laughed in his deep, rough drawl that made most women go all soft-eyed at him. "It looks like that little shit-head tried to smash the side of your face in."

Derek made a groaning noise behind his ice pack. "Yeah, well, it feels like he tried to smash it in too."

"Shit, I know this sure as hell wasn't how I'd planned on spending my night."

His buddy smiled, or at least as much as he could with his head pounding the way it was. "Don't you think you're getting a little old to be hanging out at Red Mackey's place? And God only knows it's hardly the kind of dive where an ATF guy should be seen, uh, socializing. Not unless he's undercover."

Easing back in his chair, Ryan propped his big feet on the low coffee table, crossing them at the ankles. "Red's is exactly the kinda place this particular ATF guy should be hanging out, and I'm only a year older than you, asshole."

"Hell of a difference between thirty-four and thirty-five," Derek laughed, grimacing when his split lip cracked open again.

Ryan gave him a dirty look, then with a sound somewhere between a groan and a sigh, leaned his sun-streaked head back on his chair. "Piss off, Derek."

"Hey, I'm just saying you could do a hell of a lot better than those broads you pick up at Red's. Hell, most of 'em have seen more action than I have."

Ryan was getting tired of the topic, mostly because Derek had been harping on him for the past three weeks about it. It'd become an irritating subject of conversation ever since he'd let it slip where he was spending his Friday nights, and now his tenacious, pain-in-the-ass pal wouldn't let it go. "The women at Red's go there looking for the same thing as me, so drop it. The last damn thing I need is another woman clinging to me, driving me out of my friggin' mind."

Derek snorted. "You're a cynical man, Ry."

Wide set, clear blue eyes narrowed with frustration. "Since we're on the subject of my sex life, why don't we take a look at yours, Kiely? Hannah told me you've been sniffing around her for over a week now, even asked her out to dinner for tomorrow night."

Hannah Mitchell rented the apartment directly above Shea's. When her divorce had finalized six months ago, she'd moved down from Tennessee for a chance at a new beginning. She'd known Ryan forever, having grown up with him in Nashville, and they were as close as family, even without any blood relation between them. There'd never been anything sexual about their friendship and there never would. And that fact suited Derek just fine, since he'd finally dragged his head out of the sand and taken note of what an attractive woman she was, both in character and physical appearance.

The only problem was that Hannah had been burned badly by her ex-husband, a man Derek had never met. But he knew enough from Ryan to know the guy had been bad news. *Really bad.* Now that the two-timing ass was out of the picture, Hannah wanted nothing to do with another man; especially tall, gorgeous, womanizing men like Derek Kiely. He knew because she'd told him so when he'd stopped by to ask her out on Tuesday.

Derek had stood there red-faced and irritated, and a whole hell of a lot disappointed as Hannah told him she was flattered, hoped they'd still be friends, and preferred to go on as if the entire conversation had never taken place. Then she'd smiled and closed the door in his face, leaving him standing on her doorstep like some dumb-ass idiot.

Damn. Just the memory had his voice going hard with anger. "Yeah, and before you start in on me about leaving her alone, I'm sure she told you she turned me down, so save us both the lecture."

Ryan pulled the ice away, turned it over, and reapplied it. "Who said I was going to ride you about it? So long as you're serious about her, I've been thinking you and Hannah would be kinda good together. Since her ex is out of the picture, I was wondering what was taking you so long to make a move."

Hell, Derek had wondered the same thing. "Well, it hardly matters now. But speaking of cute couples, you said yes to Shea yet?"

And just like that, Ryan went from laid-back and easy-going to stiff, tight-laced tension. Jesus, just the thought of the woman tied him in knots, not to mention what it did to his dick. "Shea? What the hell does she have to do with anything?"

Derek lifted his ice pack to send a dry look Ryan's way. "Come on, Ry. In the last two weeks, the girl has asked you to go with her to everything from the movies, to dinner, to coffee. And I've seen the way you watch her when you think nobody's looking. You're ready to throw her over your shoulder like a caveman and drag her away to your little love cave. So how come you won't give her a chance?"

He looked ready to kill. "I don't screw around with women like Shea. *So. Drop. It.*"

Derek attempted another smile, clearly enjoying the unsettled look on his normally oh-so-cool bud's face. Nothing ever rattled Ryan, but it sure as hell looked like his little next-door neighbor was rattling him but good. She was cute and sexy as hell in a kind of gypsy-like way, like something from the pages of a fairy tale. She didn't have bombshell curves, but the ones she did have were soft in that womanly way that just made a guy want to fall into her. She'd be warm and sweet as he rode her, taking everything he had to give and more, instead of feeling like he was nailing some kind of lifeless Barbie doll. Women needed to have a little give—and Ry looked more than ready to give Shea Dresden whatever the hell she wanted.

He couldn't understand what Ryan's problem was. "Why not women like Shea? What's wrong with her? She got cooties or somethin'?"

"Nothing's wrong with her, damn it," Ryan growled, tossing the pack aside and rising to his feet to pace the length of the room. "But she's too fucking young for one thing—"

Derek snorted again, cutting him off. "Come on, Ryan. She's twenty-seven. It's not like you'd be robbing the cradle."

"Damn it, Derek, the woman's just finished her dissertation on Ancient Civilizations and I spend most of my time trying to track down gutter scum. What the hell would we have in common? Hannah told me about her last two boyfriends—one was a poetry professor and the other was a fuckin' sculptor."

He kept pacing, his hands shoved in the back pockets of his jeans, jaw grinding so hard his teeth were beginning to ache. "And she's too damn innocent-looking. I set eyes on her and she blushes. God only knows what she'd do if she had a clue what I'd like to do to her."

Everything, he thought with a vicious curse. *I wanna do everything there is with her. Front, back, top, bottom. I wanna fuck her and eat that sweet little cunt until she screams herself hoarse.*

Derek raised his brow in wry amusement, as if he could read his friend's mind, still wondering what Ryan's problem was. "So what? You're not even going to give her a chance because she's young and smart and *too innocent*, whatever the hell that means? Stop being so pigheaded,

Ryan. You're not all that ancient yourself, you're too damn smart for your own good, and I hardly think she's as inexperienced as she looks. They never are. Hell, even if she was, why should that stop you?"

Ryan stalked to the window, staring out at the starless night, the black clouds mirroring his own dark mood. "Because she's not the kind of woman you fuck and move on from. Women like Shea don't expect to get tossed aside at the end of the night when you're done with them. They expect commitment and all that crap I don't believe in."

Not anymore.

Not ever again.

"Ahh," Derek drawled from the sofa. "You mean she's not like the women you find at Red's. She's looking for more, and you'd rather die than—what? Have a nice woman come to care for you? What the hell's so bad about that, especially when that woman's someone like Shea?"

Ryan whipped around with barely suppressed violence, his lip curled in disgust, though he suspected it was more with himself than with Derek. "Yeah, asks the guy who screws a different woman every weekend," he snarled. "You're sounding like a self-righteous hypocrite, Kiely."

Derek rose to his full height, matching Ryan's intimidating six-four, inch for inch. "Well at least I'm not acting like a frightened ass," he shot back, "too afraid to go out with a girl who might have more to offer than some sweaty time between the sheets."

Ryan stepped forward, his shoulders and arms bulging with muscles beneath the thin cotton of his gray T-shirt. "Just because you crashed and burned with Hannah doesn't mean you have to take this shit out on me!"

"Damn it," Derek growled, "I *did not* crash and burn."

"Huh! Only because she didn't even give you the chance to—"

They both heard, at the same time, the crash and muffled scream come through the connecting living room wall between his and Shea's apartment. Ryan's stomach knotted with dread and icy rage, while Derek muttered, "What the fuck was that?"

Another muffled scream, another thud, and suddenly Ryan sprang into action, cursing himself for standing there for even those two stunned seconds, while he'd tried to come to grips with what he'd heard. Jesus, if anyone had so much as dared to lay a hand on her, Ryan knew it was going to take a friggin' miracle to keep him from killing the sorry son-of-a-bitch.

Through a blinding fog of rage, Ryan was dimly aware of Derek moving behind him as he threw open his front door and rocketed around the building. His heart nearly stopped when he rounded the corner and saw Shea's front door busted open, the useless safety chain dangling, broken from its clasp. Without even drawing his gun, Ryan charged through the doorway, Derek right on his heels, their actions timed in perfect unison.

Another loud crash and muffled shriek had them running for the bedroom. Ryan burst through the door and stopped short. The primitive killing instinct igniting his blood all but burned through his skin, filling him with savage intent. He took one look at Rich Spalding's big body trying to pin a frantically struggling Shea to the floor and wanted to rip the man apart with his bare hands.

And Shea, God bless her, was doing her best to kick the shit out of the jerk. She had what looked like the remnants of a lamp in her hand, which she'd obviously just cracked over Spalding's thick skull. The stream of obscenities pouring from her sweet little mouth would've made the most seasoned sailor stand up and take notice.

"You fucking bastard," Ryan snarled, hauling Spalding up by the back of his shirt and tossing him clear across the room. He'd instantly recognized the big guy as one of Red's rowdier regulars. Behind him, Shea yelled his name as he started toward Spalding's sprawled form against the far wall.

Looking over his shoulder, he told Derek, "Get her the hell outta here."

Instead of agreeing, his stubborn friend just shook his dark head. "No way, Ry. As much as I'd enjoy seeing his sorry ass get pounded into the ground, you look ready to kill."

Ryan hadn't wanted to look at her yet, knowing he wasn't going to be able to deal with it if she was hurt, but Shea stumbled in front of him, grasping on to his arm, demanding his attention.

"Damn it, Ryan, calm down! He's not worth it. Just arrest him," she all but shouted in his face. It took all her effort not to throw her arms around the beautiful man and thank him, from his golden head down to his big feet, but first she had to keep him from committing murder in her bedroom. "I mean it, Ryan. I don't want you killing his sorry ass because of me."

He looked down into her tear-streaked face, seeing the small cut at the corner of her bruised mouth and the slight swelling on her right cheekbone. New fury blazed within his battle-readied body, making him shake with it. Even his fingers trembled as they reached out to brush her swollen lip, stopping just short of touching her.

"Damn it, Shea. That bastard hurt you. God only knows what he would've done if I hadn't come home and heard you fighting him. No way in hell am I letting him walk away from this."

Spalding, who'd been leaning against the wall trying to get his breath back, chose that moment to try and make a run for it. As he shot past them, Ryan reached out and caught the front of his shirt, lifted him clear off his feet, and slammed his fist into the asshole's nose. There was an awful crunching sound, and then Ryan tossed him to the floor where he lay in a motionless heap. Blood poured unchecked down the guy's swelling face, collecting under his beefy chin.

Derek walked over, tossed down his denim jacket to protect Shea's carpet, then nudged Spalding to his stomach with his foot so he could handcuff him and keep the drunken lout from choking on his own blood. While he fastened the cuffs, he ignored Ryan, who still stood glowering down at Spalding's unconscious body, clearly spoiling for another go at the bastard, and instead focused his attention on Shea. She stood beside Ryan with a stunned look of shock and outrage on her pale face, as if she didn't know whether to throw her arms around his dumb-ass pal or run screaming from the room.

Derek understood Ryan's violent reaction. Hell, he wanted a go at Spalding himself, but Shea needed some attention before she collapsed at Ryan's feet. Hannah would've been the ideal choice, but she'd driven up to her mother's yesterday and wouldn't be back until Sunday night. That left it up to him, since Ryan was looking about as gentle as a raging bull.

Trying to put her at ease, he gave her a slow smile. "You okay, honey? You need me to call an ambulance?"

She shook her head no, her dazed eyes darting between him and Ryan. "Okay," he said in that same easy way, as if he were dealing with a skittish animal. "You want to go ahead and tell me what happened? Then I can get him outta here and let you get settled. I'll come back tomorrow and take your statement."

"Like hell you will," Ryan muttered, cutting off whatever it was she was about to say. Ignoring the sudden glare she sent him, he explained roughly, "I'll take her damn statement myself."

Derek hid his knowing smile by looking down to check the cuffs. "Hey, whatever you want, Ry."

Ryan didn't even reply. His attention had been completely captured by Shea. She looked about ready to fall on her face, and the anger rolled through him hotter than ever.

"What happened, Shea?" He tried to gentle his voice, but there was no disguising the simmering violence just waiting to be unleashed. She didn't seem to be afraid, though, not if the burning daggers she was sending his way were any indication, her small finger suddenly poking him painfully in the chest.

"*You…big…arrogant…macho…idiot!* Just what in the hell did you think you were doing?"

Behind him, Derek made an odd choking sound, one Ryan strongly suspected was caused by swallowed laughter, and tried to figure out what had the gorgeous little imp in front of him in such a snit. He figured she'd be shaken after an attempted rape, damn it, but he sure as hell hadn't expected to have her chewing a strip off his own hide. He was the one who'd saved her sweet little ass and all she could do was screech at him?

"What did I think I was doing?" he sneered, looming over her until she had to crane her neck back to see his face. "How about saving your scrawny, ungrateful, bitchy little backside? Jesus, Shea, what the hell's the matter with you?"

The Shea he knew was sweet and shy and so far out of his league it wasn't even funny. He didn't know who the hell the little sexpot standing in front of him was, giving as good as she got, but his dick was standing up and taking notice, and Ryan felt ready to strangle the damn thing in frustration.

She took one deep breath, then another, her small nostrils flaring as she struggled to calm down and stop shrieking like a fishwife. "Okay, look, I don't mean to sound ungrateful. You were bloody brilliant and you know it. Just don't go acting like you're going to commit a homicide over me because of some stupid, drunk asshole, whose balls I was about to shove down his throat. God, Ry, I thought you were going to rip his heart out there for a second, and I don't want you thrown into jail along with him!"

"You've got a pretty screwed up way of saying thanks, Shea."

"Well you almost scared me as much as he did." Then, with a small smile that he felt all the way down to his dick, she arched one fine brow and said, "Maybe I should just shut up now and say thank you." Her eyes darkened and she took a step closer to him, one that had Ryan stumbling back a quick step. "How can I say it and make sure you believe me, Ry? I wouldn't want you to think I'm ungrateful."

His gut cramped and he swallowed hard, thinking of the dozens of ways he'd have loved to have her sweet little body thanking him...sucking him...screwing him into sexual oblivion. Unfortunately, he and the delectable Shea Dresden were never going to happen. Not tonight. Not ever.

But she was so fucking soft. He loved the way the mellow light in her bedroom played over the surface of her skin. Loved the soft, sensual lines of her body, and the sexy little silver hoop he knew was nestled in her navel beneath the silky blackness of her dress. It was the best damn part of his day, whenever he was lucky enough to catch a glimpse of her in her blue bikini and see that little silver hoop glinting brightly against her golden skin.

And her hands. Hell, he was in some serious shit when he started mooning over a woman's hands. But Shea's hands were so damn sexy. They were soft and smooth, with little dimples on her knuckles that he just wanted to brush with his lips, and then drag her pretty little hand down to his cock, where she could wrap those delicate fingers around the pulsing mass of his erection.

She always made him so painfully hard—he just wanted to freaking explode with it. He had a sudden vision of Shea on her knees, her lips parted as she swallowed his cock, his hot cum shooting down her throat while she sucked on him with her greedy little tongue and lips.

Oh, damn, that was a good one. But still not the best. No—the best was having her under him, all quivering and wet and soft, while he pounded his cock into her like a hammer and drilled her into one screaming climax after another. He'd pump harder and harder, cramming her to the hilt until she was packed full and ready to burst around him...until he was ramming himself into the depths of her soul, and then he'd unload into her like a flood. He'd mark her as his own—fill her full of his seed—and keep her forever...

Whoa! Where in the fuck did that come from? Shit, he didn't want her forever—he just wanted her now! Just wanted to be able to screw this insane need for her out of his system once and for all. Just needed to get his cock in that hot little cunt and burn the need for her from his body before it drove him friggin' nuts.

Forcing his traitorous mind back on track, Ryan tried again. "The, ah, words are just fine, Shea, but I want you to tell me what happened here." He jerked his head toward the floor, where Spalding's body lay reeking of alcohol and sweat and blood. "Do you know this guy?"

Shea frowned down at the unconscious heap on her floor, looking as if she might enjoy giving him another good kick. Ryan thought she just might, too, considering she'd fought the bastard like a hellcat. Half of Spalding's face had long ugly scratches, probably from her nails, and he'd limped when he'd tried to run as if she'd kneed him in the nuts. All in all, she'd put up a damn good fight, and now she genuinely seemed more angry than upset.

Still, it made Ryan's blood run cold to think of what would've happened if he hadn't heard her. No way in hell would he have been able to live with it if anything had happened to her. He didn't know how the hell it had happened, but she'd come to mean so much to him, even though he'd fought it. Shit, he was still fighting it.

How had she gotten under his skin?

What had she done to him?

And what in God's name was he going to do about her now?

Shea's next words ripped Ryan out of his personal, private ramblings, hitting him like a punch in the gut. "I don't know him, but I saw him tonight at Red Mackey's Bar. He started to bother me there, but this pretty redhead who works there stepped in and told him to leave me alone. I left after that, but I guess he must've followed me home," she added with a small frown, shivering from the memory of when he'd pushed his way in through her door.

In those brief moments, she'd been furious, able to think of nothing else but kicking the bejesus out of the jerk until Ryan could come and really give him hell. Somehow she'd just known he would. Her hero, though she knew it'd be a cold day in hell before he'd ever admit it.

Hannah had been feeding her stories of Ryan's heroic deeds for weeks now, just like a proud mother. Shea had heard everything from how he'd once found a three-year-old who'd been abducted, to the case involving a terrorist Ryan had taken down in a knife fight. After learning so much about him, her downright carnal lust was swiftly evolving into something much stronger — and so much more frightening.

She not only wanted Ryan, but she respected him as well. More than any other person she'd ever known. Without any means of protecting her heart, she'd made herself unbearably vulnerable and fallen helplessly in love with the magnificent jerk. Hard and fast and head over heels.

Glancing up at his rugged face, Shea realized, with a muffled groan, that he looked even more furious than before. *Well, hell.* By mentioning Red's, she'd definitely let the cat outta the bag. She'd wanted him panting with lust tonight, not shaking with rage.

"What in God's name were you doing at Red Mackey's Bar?" he exploded, staring at her as if she'd grown a second head. "Jesus Christ, woman, are you out of your mind? Do you know what could've happened to you there?" He shot a disgusted look down at Spalding, then snapped his angry glare back on her. "Forget *could* have. Look what *did* happen because you went there!"

Shea stared up at him in silence, not knowing what to say, especially with Derek standing there watching them. She didn't exactly care for his condescending tone, but she thought it might have more to do with fear than anything else, so she was willing to let it slide for the moment. He looked so scared and angry at the thought of what she might've suffered at the hands of Rich Spalding, and she couldn't help but love him even more for his concern.

And maybe it meant that he cared—even if just a little. She'd have loved to press him for more details, but there wasn't much she could say with Derek still in the room, not to mention the grotesque drunk on her floor.

As if he read her mind, Ryan's tall, good-looking friend hefted Spalding over his shoulder. "Look," he said, trying to hold back a grin, "if you two promise to behave yourselves, I'll haul this piece of sh—er, crap on down to the station."

Ryan nodded mechanically, unable to tear his eyes away from the picture Shea presented in her slinky black dress and sexy sandals, driving himself crazy thinking of how she must have stuck out in a place like Red's. He watched as she told Derek thank you, and felt an unfamiliar burst of jealousy to see the blush on her cheeks when his pain-in-the-ass buddy winked at her on his way out.

And suddenly, for the first time ever, they were alone, in her bedroom no less, and Christ Almighty, he was gonna get hard just staring at her. Ryan supposed he should be used to that particular reaction by now, which was nothing new whenever Shea was anywhere near the vicinity of his dick. In fact, he tended to get a raging hard-on every damn time he saw her.

Judging by the effect she was having on him right now, he was uncomfortably aware of the fact that fighting this thing between them tonight was going to be harder than ever before. Hell, she looked like a woman on the prowl for a wild night, and Ryan knew he wanted to be the man to give it to her. He wanted to give it to her every way there was, from every conceivable angle, and if she were any other woman, they'd already be halfway there. Shit, since setting eyes on her, he'd imagined every woman he'd fucked was Shea Dresden. He'd fantasized it was her sweet little pussy he was pounding into instead of whatever woman he was with at the time.

He wanted her so damn bad it was killing him.

But this was shy, sweet, studious Shea, Hannah's new best friend and his naïve little neighbor—the only woman who'd ever made him nervous and aching for just a glimpse of her. *Jesus.* The thought of actually sinking into her, of spreading those smooth, golden legs that he knew would open up to the sweetest pair of cunt lips he'd ever tasted, was enough to make him tremble, damn it.

With perfect clarity, he remembered the first time he'd ever seen her. She'd been walking by his patio with Hannah, the two of them wearing bikinis on their way back from the pool where they'd only just met. Shea's suit had been a deep, dark blue with a matching skirt thing tied around her narrow waist. It'd been all he could do to pay attention as Hannah had introduced her, explaining how Shea had only just moved in the day before.

Ryan had been dumbstruck by his reaction to the delicate young woman, barely able to peel his tongue off the roof of his mouth to make the appropriate polite conversation. Then she'd smiled at him—her big gray eyes sparkling, her impish nose slightly sunburned, a dimple in her right cheek—and he'd thought she was the most beautiful thing he'd ever seen.

And in her sweet little navel had been this glinting little spark of light. He'd tried to get a better view without looking as if he was staring at the shining silver hoop nestled there, but he'd probably done a piss poor job of it. Funny, but he'd never really gone for the whole piercing thing before Shea. But there had been something incredibly erotic about seeing that little hoop of silver pierced through her skin. He'd wanted to press a kiss against it, dip his tongue into the shallow indentation of her navel, and then flick the silver hoop.

Hell, he'd wanted to drag her into his apartment and kiss and lick and suck on her golden little body from head to toe. His mouth had watered for a taste of those tiny nipples that had hardened beneath the wet material of her suit, his tongue itching for a long lick inside her juice-soaked pussy, and his cock had gone rock-hard thinking of all the ways he'd fuck her if given half the chance.

Ryan had felt lust often enough to know what it was. As an aggressively dominant male, he'd always enjoyed a healthy sexual appetite, one that was probably stronger than most. Yeah, he'd felt lust and he'd satisfied it, but he'd *never* felt anything like his volatile reaction to Shea. It'd unsettled him, and he'd been trying to avoid it, running from it, ever since.

She'd made him feel like a teenage boy trapped in the uncomfortable, yet exciting throes of lust. Hell, he still felt that way.

And now, here he was, alone with her in her bedroom, her champagne lace-covered bed not five feet away, with her staring up at him like she wanted to eat him alive. Every single friggin' inch of him. His jaw hardened, his stomach cramped with need, and his cock grew harder. Ryan closed his eyes and did something he hadn't done since he was a little boy. He prayed.

He begged whoever was listening for the strength to resist the one thing in his adult life he'd ever really wanted.

Chapter Two

The glow from Shea's bedside lamp was soft and low, casting tall shadows against the book-lined walls and antique furnishings of her room. It was an intimate setting, and one Ryan couldn't wait to escape.

When he'd regained some modicum of control, he opened his eyes and glared down at her. He was determined to intimidate some sense into the infuriating woman, and equally determined to ignore how she looked standing before him, her sumptuous little body all but half-naked in that damn dress. "What the hell were you doing in a place like Red's, Shea? Do you even know what kind of people hang out there?"

Even if she didn't, he sure as hell did, and knowing all too well of the danger she'd been in had his blood boiling.

With her chin stubbornly raised, she glared right back up at him, ignoring his ferocious scowl. "Yeah, I know what kind of people go to Red Mackey's for entertainment. Unless I'm mistaken, which I'm not, you hang out there all the time, Ry."

"Damn it," he gritted through his clenched teeth, wondering why she was pushing him. Where had his shy little scholar gone? The one who turned strawberry pink every time he looked at her, trying to imagine what her naked body would look like spread out across his sheets, arms and legs secured to the posts, while he ate his way to heaven. With the way she smelled, she would have to be the sweetest tongue-fuck he'd ever had. He'd fantasized about it so many damn times he could almost taste it, as if she were already slipping across his tongue, sliding down his throat like honey.

Only...he wasn't ever really going to have her, was he? And knowing it had him feeling meaner than hell. "Listen, Shea, that's different and you know it."

"Is it?" she purred. His gut cramped at the sound. This low, breathless tone was one he'd never heard from her before. It sounded suspiciously seductive, as if she were coming on to him. His fear took on a new dimension, one that embarrassingly resembled blind fucking terror. "Why, Ry? Maybe I went there looking for the same thing you do."

Ah hell, he thought with a sharp rise of panic. Did she even know how close to disaster she was flirting? How close he was to forgetting all the reasons why he couldn't give her exactly what they both apparently wanted? How close he was to finally burying his cock up her cunt, right where it'd been dying to get since he'd first set eyes on her?

Shit—he wanted her in ways he'd never before experienced—wanted all of her. Everything.

She wasn't classically beautiful, but then he'd never been the kind of man attracted to Barbie doll perfection. At least not since he was old enough to know better. One Barbie doll had cured him for life, and it wasn't a lesson he'd ever forget.

No, Shea's was a face of exotic angles and planes, from her small nose to her wide, lush mouth, thick lashes and arched brows. She looked like a sylvan creature stolen from a primeval forest—a pixie siren—with those wild black curls streaming around her face and her sharp little chin.

Ryan scrubbed his hands down his whisker-rough face, feeling as if he were dangerously close to losing control of the situation. Then again, maybe he'd never had it in the first place. This entire night was turning into one hell-inspired carnival ride. Shit, he'd get a better dose of reality from a friggin' funhouse mirror. All of this was just as surreal, distorting his point-of-view. If he had to stare at her in that little fuck-me outfit for much longer, he was going to forget all the reasons why she was off-limits. He'd be all over her, crammed deep inside before he knew what hit him, and the consequences of that were too damn dangerous for his peace of mind.

"Look, Shea, when I go there—I mean when guys like me go to Red's—we're not looking to hook up with some nice girl, not with someone like you," he struggled to explain, knowing he was making a muck of it, but unable to stop the idiotic ramble spilling out of his mouth. "The women go there looking for the same thing, and I know that's not the speed you run at, honey. You've got sweet and innocent stamped all over you."

"Yeah?" she asked with wide-eyed speculation, as if she didn't know exactly what she was doing to him. "Hmm...you know, maybe you don't know me as well as you think, Ry. You've heard the old saying, 'you can't always judge a book by its cover,' haven't you?"

He didn't bother with an answer, grinding his jaw instead, struggling to keep from gripping her slim shoulders and shaking some sense into her.

But his expression told her everything she needed to know. With a small, frustrated smile, she turned and walked away from him.

He hated this. Hated being this close to her because it took so much effort to control himself. Too much effort to act as if he didn't want to toss her over his shoulder and spend the next fifty years of his life showing her sweet, innocent little ass all the things he'd been dying to do to her since the moment they'd met.

Most of all, though, Ryan hated the uncomfortable feeling of longing she stirred within him, the kind that damn near made his heart stutter whenever she was near. Honest to God, he didn't know how much longer he could hold out against it. Each and every time he laid eyes on her, his legendary control slipped a little further. And after tonight, it was tenuous as hell, riddled with cracks.

Shea stared out the window, trying not to let it hurt that he was struggling so damn hard. She could try to be as tough as she liked, but there was no denying the fact that if she didn't get Ryan McCall buried deep inside of her at the soonest possible moment, it was going to damn near kill her. That, or drive her out of her ever-loving mind. Inside she was a jumble of rioting emotion—her fierce determination and desire battling against the infuriating realization that he was going to fight her to the bitter end.

She had to figure out how to get through to him, because she wasn't willing to go through life never knowing how incredible it felt to be wrapped up in his muscled arms, to have him wrapped up in her body, to feel him inside of her, so vital and honest and real.

She could have had a score of other lovers by now, but that wasn't what she'd wanted. She wanted to be taken by a *real* man, and Ryan McCall was the most *real* man she'd ever known, in every way. After falling so hard for him, no other guy was going to do.

But what were her options here? Why did he keep putting up such a struggle?

Screwing up her courage to confess everything, Shea felt him come up behind her, not close enough to touch — *he never touched her* — but near enough that she could sense him there. She looked up at the darkened window and could see his rugged reflection rising above her own, so tall and rough and gorgeous. Not perfect — but still the most amazing person she'd ever known.

When he spoke, his voice was quiet, deep, sending goose bumps across her flesh from the sound alone. "Why'd you go there, Shea? What did you really think you were going to find in a place like that?"

Her eyes met his in the glass, gray against blue, the stormy sea and the midnight sky. She stood on the edge of a cliff, arms flung wide, and jumped. "You, Ryan. God, don't you get it? I went there to find *you*. Who else do you think I was looking for?"

Ryan frowned, and this time there was an edge to his voice that she'd never quite heard before. Not anger really, but more like...like desperation. "Looking for me to do what, damn it?"

Shea's eyes closed, her lips curving in bitter amusement. Her heart was broken, but hey, at least she could still laugh at herself. "I went there to pick you up, Ry. Come on, is it really so hard to get the concept?"

The frown remained, the look in his eyes telling her he wasn't quite buying it when she peeked a look at his expression. Or maybe he just found it too ridiculous to believe.

She couldn't help it. She laughed slightly, a soft sound only partly humor, and hugged her arms around her body, holding herself together. She looked back out through the glass, losing her gaze to the safe blackness of the night. "Is it really so hard to believe? I knew that's where you picked up your...*women.* Hannah told me all about your little Friday night excursions. And I also knew that if I was ever going to...to...*oh hell*—" She paused to take a deep breath, and then slowly let it out. "I knew that if I was ever going to get your attention—"

Strong hands clamped down on her shoulders, spinning her around, pressing her back up against the cool panes of the window with a small push. Her breath hitched, stopping the flow of her confession, and suddenly there was no more air to draw in to finish it. One look at the heat in his eyes and every word curled in on itself in her mind, like paper within a flame.

"Ryan?" she asked breathlessly, hating the way he was looking at her with so much resentment firing his beautiful stare.

"What the hell are you talking about, Shea? Are you crazy?" he gritted through his clenched teeth, every word bitten and hard with fury.

His eyes went darker, as if that were possible, and slowly traveled down the length of her scantily clad body, sending a rush of heat through her blood. Her own chin lifted with stubborn pride. "You may not like it, but it's the truth. I went there because I thought—"

"You thought what, you little idiot? That I'd pick you up in a place like Red's and that would make it okay for me to fuck you?" he demanded crudely, trying to hurt her. Anything to scare her away before he did the unthinkable and gave in to what his damn cock wanted so badly.

"I—" She swallowed thickly, working for her voice, knowing she'd rather die than back down now. "I've tried everything, Ryan, but you never give me a chance. It's like you see right through me, like I'm not even there! So yeah, I thought seeing me at Red Mackey's Bar might make you think of me differently, and really notice who I am. What's so wrong with that? You go to bed with the rest of them. *Why not with me?*"

He was so angry he felt like he wanted to rip something apart—so friggin' on edge that all he really wanted was to plow his aching cock up her pussy and take everything he'd wanted to take for the past three godforsaken months. What was she trying to do to him?

As if watching through a thick fog of physical need, he saw one big hand move from her shoulder to her breast. He fingered the sensuous silk covering the firm mound and deliberately rasped her small nipple, trying desperately to ignore what the feel of her did to his dick. At this rate, he was going to reach ungodly proportions.

"And this?" he asked with a forced, cocky smirk, ruefully aware that the simple touch of her nipple beneath his fingertips was about to make him come in his pants. "Was this get-up supposed to make me want you, Shea? Make me see you as anything other than a naïve young woman asking for something she wouldn't know what to do with in the first place? I'm not one of your young poets or artists, damn it. When I take a woman home for the night, it's not all rosy and sweet. I fuck with my mouth and my hands and my cock, with the lights bright, honey, so I can see just what kind of cunt I'm pounding into. I'm not soft and I'm sure as hell not small, and I don't think you really know what you want. Christ, I'm twice your size," he sneered. "I'd probably tear you apart!"

Oh God, she silently groaned, feeling a rush of liquid heat melt her pussy at his shocking touch and words. She swallowed over the lump in her throat and tried to find a spark of hope in the fear she'd heard just beneath his anger. "No, you're wrong, damn it. I know what I want. You're just too afraid to believe it. What is it, Ry? You got a thing about not sleeping with anyone who knows more about you than your first name?"

His eyes widened, then narrowed, pinning her in place — something shifting through them that she didn't understand, couldn't identify. "So you went there to get laid, huh?"

He took her left nipple between two knuckles and twisted the small nub, eliciting a sharp breath from her parted, wine-colored lips. The warm look in her gray gaze became glazed with desire, stormy and vague, as if she were already on the verge of coming, and he knew she'd be one of those women he could bring to orgasm just by sucking on her tits. "I hadn't pegged you as that kind of girl, but then, hey — I've been wrong before."

Shea couldn't think of an argument, not with the barrage of emotions and physical sensations spearing through her. All she could think to give him was the truth. "I went there looking for you, Ryan. Because I want you." She swallowed, panted — pleaded with the hungry look in her eyes. "Because I want you to want me the same way."

He smiled at that, but there was no joy in it, no warmth. Without taking his eyes from hers, he reached behind her to draw the blinds, then closed his large hands over her bare shoulders. With insistent pressure, he easily maneuvered her to the side until the smooth surface of the wall was at her back. When he had her where he wanted her, he let go.

"Well, I'm here now," he drawled in a husky rasp. "If you want me to give it to you, Shea, get rid of the clothes."

"What?" she asked blankly, not quite following his sudden change in mood. One minute he was pissed at her—and in the next he wanted to have sex?

"You heard me. Strip that pathetic excuse for a dress from this little body and I'll think about giving you the screwing you went looking for tonight."

Shea stiffened, instinctively trying to pull away at his snide tone, but a big hand gripped her arm, holding her in place. "Last chance, Shea. Take it off now or don't ever come near me again."

Ryan was calling her bluff. It was a challenge. She could see it in his eyes and the grim set of his mouth. Shea understood that much and she also believed him. And she wanted him enough to go through with it. Wanted him enough to hope that somehow she'd reach him this way, when every other way had failed.

You can do this…you can do this…you can *do this!*

She silently repeated the litany over and over, determined to see this through, no matter how daunting the idea seemed of stripping naked in front of him while he stood before her completely clothed and acting like an ass. She *had* to see this through, because no way in hell was she willing to give up on him now.

Forget her heart. Forget how she felt about him. Forget the emotions involved. She owed this to her poor, sex-starved body. Owed it the fuck of a lifetime, and Ryan McCall was the perfect man for the job.

For the first time in her life, she was going to be the one having all the fun—the one getting the stud instead of the dud. Her one pathetic attempt at sex had been the biggest screw-up in the history of screwing, because she'd been so busy listening to her mind, she hadn't heard her body.

But she was listening to it now. And it told her that Ryan McCall made Jimmy Prescott look like a limp-dicked little prick with peach pits for balls.

Oh yeah, she'd made a bad decision the first time around, mostly from letting stupid fear dictate her actions. *Hey Shea...you gotta get a guy. And Shea...you better make sure it's a guy you can handle.* So she had, only to end up with Jimmy, who'd cared more about messing up his hair than getting her off. And then it'd been *Whoa, Shea...you must've been out of your friggin' mind!*

Right there—the story of her life. So much time wasted waiting for what she wanted to come to her. Too many years spent living like a nun, hiding behind her fears and labels. Too many nights spent alone, when she should've dragged her head out of the sand ages ago and opened her eyes to a world of sensual possibilities.

Of course, it wasn't until Ryan had flashed her that lopsided grin of his that she'd truly understood what she'd been missing out on. And now that she knew, she was ready to know a whole hell of a lot more, no matter how much of a warning her heart was screaming at her.

No snotty-nosed little dickhead for her this time around. *Oh no.* Her body had chosen a guy with enough explosive, dominating sexuality to keep her pulsing with pleasure until she passed out—and Shea was looking forward to every single decadent second of it.

He wasn't a pretty-boy piece of eye-candy, and she liked that. For the life of her, Shea had never been able to understand Hollywood's obsession with androgynous men. *Bleck!* What woman in her right mind wanted to go out with a guy who was prettier than she was? No, there wasn't anything pretty about Ryan, but he was beautiful in an entirely masculine sort of way. A tall, golden bad boy with sinful looks and a wicked reputation.

He moved with the menacing ease of a dangerous predator, and Shea had gone to bed every night wondering if he moved the same way when lying between a woman's thighs, buried deep within her body, fucking her brains out.

But even with her vivid imagination, she knew her limited experience could in no way do him justice. It would be like comparing rotten apples to Chocolate Sin Cake. No, his sexual prowess was something she was just going to have to find out for herself, and she and her sex-starved libido were more than ready for the opportunity.

They were ready for it right now.

She looked up at him from beneath her long lashes and suddenly her lips curled into a wicked smile full of carnal possibilities, feral and hungry and *God-it's-about-time!* Then with trembling fingers, she pushed the silky dress right off her shoulders. It fell to the floor in a quiet swoosh of fabric, and she was standing before him wearing nothing but a miniscule black lace thong and her sandals.

Ryan felt his stomach drop to his feet and his heart lodge in his throat. *Oh, hell.* The last of his control shot to pieces as the raging hunger she always ignited in him blazed to life. He'd fought for so long to keep it tightly bottled up with denial, and now he staggered under its force. What was it about this woman that drove him to this, that pushed him so far beyond any place he'd ever been before?

He tried to think of what to say. Something...*anything*, but there were no words, nothing to hold on to over the frantic pumping of his blood. He stared down at her, his eyes wild with need. Her breasts were somewhat small but beautiful, incredibly sexy and perfectly shaped with pink-tipped, uplifted nipples that he wanted to lick and suck and tease with the scrape of his teeth. Every raw, dirty, sexually explicit act he'd fantasized about doing to her burned through his brain in a torrent of erotic images, making him quiver with lust.

His gaze lowered and his eyes found the dark triangle of curls through the sheer black panel of her panties, and he could just make out the delicate cleft of her cunt. More than anything in the world, Ryan wanted to press his face there, separate her lips with his thumbs, and plunge his tongue deep inside of her until she filled his mouth with her taste. He wanted to make her scream and claw and beg until he'd impressed himself on her so thoroughly, they couldn't be torn apart.

It was terrifying.

And sheer freaking insanity!

His cock swelled to the point that he feared he'd bust straight through the fly of his jeans just from looking at her. Then everything happened at once. One second he was staring down at her with glittering blue eyes—and in the next, he was all over her.

Chapter Three

As if they had a mind of their own, Ryan's fingers gripped Shea's tightly, his intention clearly to stop her if she tried to pull away. But she wasn't trying. Just as she'd hoped, his free hand swiftly ripped open the fly of his jeans. His movements were jerky and urgent as he thrust her hand through his open fly, filling her small palm with the brutal thickness of his pulsing cock.

He was unbelievable, so incredibly long and strong and thicker than anything she'd ever imagined.

Somehow she'd always envisioned him fitting into her hand the way Jimmy had, instead of overflowing with so many inches of hard, thick flesh. She knew there was no logical way she could ever take all of him inside her.

Dear God, just the thought made Shea flush with heat. This couldn't be normal, could it? All she had, besides what she'd read about, was a measly point of comparison with a guy who'd made her feel like a sex-ed demo: just insert tab A into slot B and try not to fall asleep before it's all over. Not that she could've ever fallen asleep in the sixty seconds it'd taken Jimmy to get it in, bump between her legs with the finesse of a dog dry-humping someone's leg, and then blow his load in his rubber while groaning, "Oh baby, Jimmy gives it so good."

Puh...lease. She'd been so revolted she'd grabbed her things, headed back to her dorm room, and immediately taken an hour long, scalding shower to wash the whole sordid experience away.

But Ryan was just as intoxicating as she'd always known he would be. All she wanted to do was get closer to him, until they were smashed against one another, and she could feel all that delicious strength and heat pounding her—inside of her. Damn, even through the barrier of his cotton boxers, his skin was hot to the touch—and hotter still as he forced down the elastic waistband. Then she was touching him flesh to flesh and couldn't bite back the low hum of arousal that burst from her throat.

Ryan's big body shuddered against her slight frame as he worked her fingers up and down the length of his aching cock, his own hand showing her how to touch him, how hard he liked to be gripped and pulled.

With his face suddenly buried in the sensitive crook of her neck and shoulder, Shea could feel the harsh groans of breath bursting from his throat against her skin, so warm and exciting. She loved the silkiness of his flesh, the burgeoning, granite-hard mass of pumping blood buried beneath the sliding skin.

"*Oh fuck*," he muttered, and again he guided her motions, teaching her how to stroke him from root to tip, their fingers tangled around the huge, pulsing rod.

When Shea felt the moisture gathering on the massive, plum-like head, she couldn't resist the erotic urge to explore the weeping slit with her thumb. "You're wet," she murmured thickly, smearing the pearly drops across the broad crown.

Ryan ground his forehead into the wall above her left shoulder, pumping his cock between their fingers while animal-like snarls escaped his throat. He was hard and thick, pulsing from the wide base all the long way up to the huge head, and her sweet little touches were damn near unmanning him. His free hand fisted, then slammed into the wall beside his head. "Christ," he panted gruffly. "I need to touch you, Shea, but I don't wanna rush this — *rush you*."

"Damn it, Ryan, do I look rushed?" She loved his warm, masculine scent and nuzzled his collarbone for more. But she needed his taste too, and so she lapped at the hollow in the base of his throat, wanting to explore everywhere at once. "Please touch me, Ry. I've dreamed about what it'd be like to have your hands on me, inside of me, making me scream."

He cursed viciously beneath his breath, and before she could blink, he ripped the insubstantial black lace thong from her body.

Her empty hand was taken from its resting place against his hard-muscled chest. This time she suffered a moment's hesitation as he forced it between her own legs, his fingers relentless in their hold and deliberate intent, their other hands still stroking his cock.

She squirmed against him, shocked and flushed and so hungry for him she could barely stay on her feet. An excited moan broke through her lips as Ryan kneed her legs farther apart and moved their fingers across her drenched pussy, allowing her to feel the slippery wet heat and swollen flesh.

"God, I want to fuck you," he groaned against her neck, his face buried there, breathing in her sultry, feminine scent with every ragged breath he took.

The back of her head ground into the wall and her eyes squeezed tightly shut. "Uhhmm —"

He'd said he wanted to fuck her, and that's what she wanted too, more than anything, but somehow this was all moving so fast and she was suddenly finding herself more anxious than she'd actually thought she'd be. Ryan was as sexually experienced as a guy could get, and even though she had a good grasp of the fundamentals, there was still so much that she'd never experienced in real time — beyond the realm of her sexual fantasies. What if he could tell? What if she did something that clued him in and sent him running again?

As if he sensed the jumble of emotions roaring through her sensory-overloaded system, he grunted, "It's okay, Shea. You're fine. Don't fight it, honey. You feel how wet you are? How swollen your little cunt lips feel?" His voice had gone rough with awe, thick with need. "You really do want me, don't you?"

The evidence of just how much she wanted him was drenching their fingers, making her swollen pussy hot and slick with cream. Ryan left no part of her untouched, as if he were greedy for it all, every slick surface and texture. His hands moved hers, fingers guiding fingers, slow and knowingly. Then his long, rough middle finger penetrated the tiny opening of her body, working its way up through the wonderfully constricting tightness of her cunt.

His groan was long, deep — almost pain-filled — and he didn't stop until he had it buried up to his palm.

Shea made no sound at all, afraid one soft sigh or fractured breath would shatter her into a million pieces. She'd never imagined just having his finger shoved inside of her could feel so...so...*intense*. So full. Her muscles were clenching deep inside, clamping down on him, desperate for more. It felt so different than when Jimmy had touched her — so much fuller, richer, hotter.

"You're like a wet little mouth squeezing my finger, Shea. I've never felt anything so tight and wet. Shit, it must've been a long time for you, huh?" he muttered angrily, working his big finger out and back in, still trapping her own hand beneath his palm, grinding it against her clit. "Is that why you want me in here? Why you're willing to lower yourself and let me cram my hungry cock into this creamy cunt—because it's been too damn long since you were fucked raw?"

The callous words burned, but Shea knew what he was doing. Ryan liked his walls, and he was tough enough to fight dirty, even now, to keep them intact. He was willing to be ugly and crude to keep her from breaking through and reaching him. But she hadn't come this far to let him get away from her now. Swallowing her frustration, she said, "It's not going to work this time, Ry. You're not going to scare me away and hurt my feelings, so give it up."

The hand trapped beneath his twisted until she was able to reverse positions and grip his own, forcing his finger even deeper, making them both moan. "I want you here," she told him in a husky whisper, moving her hips, "because it's where you belong. You know it's true. You've just been too damn stubborn to admit it."

That hit too close to the truth, and so he fought back the only way he knew how. "What were you really looking for, Shea?" His tone was snide as he leaned back and gave her a deliberately lewd look, thrusting a second large finger into her, knowing it was too much for the narrow slit to take. Her taut flesh was stretched and straining, quivering from his penetration. "Did you want what Rich Spalding was dishing out? Is that what turns you on, honey? You want a man big enough to get rough with you?"

Shea shivered, but she didn't back down. "You don't scare me, so stop trying. I know you'd never hurt a woman. You can call me names because you're angry or afraid, but it's not going to send me running, Ry. There's no way in hell you could ever hurt me."

His eyes blazed. "If you really believe that, then you're even more naïve than you look. I'd never physically hurt you on purpose, that's true—but if you're expecting anything more from me than this, then you *are* going to get hurt!"

Her mouth opened to launch another argument, but Ryan twisted his fingers and jammed them into a sweet spot buried deep inside of her, bringing instead a sharp gasp from between her lips. Then his thumb found her stiff clit, brushing it so softly she thought her heart would stop.

"But you're just going to have to deal with it, because I'm through fighting this thing between us." His mouth pressed against hers, rough and insistent, the words grunted against her lips. *"And I'm not afraid of you."*

"The hell you aren't!" She pulled back to see his face, and the knowing look in her big gray eyes was all woman. It scared the hell out of him.

"I wish I knew why. Whatever happened to you before, I'm not—I'd never hurt you. I lo—"

The words were cut off as quickly as they'd tumbled forth, lost beneath the hungry assault of his mouth as it slashed across hers. His jaws worked as he moved his head from one angle to another, testing the fit of their mouths, forcing her to let him deeper. His tongue stroked her lips, her teeth, then arrowed to the back of her throat, tasting her completely, as if he'd eat her alive. As if he couldn't get quite deep enough into her.

Now the sexy growls he made, so savage and raw, were thrust deep into her mouth while he stroked and penetrated, demanding everything from her.

For a moment Shea was lost, drowning beneath the hungry demands of his lips and tongue, her heart beating like a maddened thing ready to burst through her chest. His taste was incredible, like honey and cinnamon, making her crave more and more. She wanted to drink him in until she was drunk on him, until he'd filled all the empty hollows of her life with his warm, sexy flavor.

Suddenly their wet fingers were pulling at his clothes, and together they somehow managed to pull his T-shirt over his head, all but ripping the seams in their urgency. When he pressed his bare chest against her naked breasts, she thought she'd die from the pleasure of it. His golden brown chest hair, slightly darker than that on his head, chafed against her sensitive nipples and they instantly hardened into two distinct little points, stabbing into the sculpted wall of muscle.

Ryan's mouth broke from hers long enough for him to lower his head and take one pretty pink nipple into the biting wet suction of his mouth. A raw cry of need rushed from her, answered by his own gruff sound of arousal as he ate at her plump breast, his jaws and throat working to take her in.

Just when Shea thought she couldn't take the exquisite torture a moment longer, Ryan moved to her other breast, laving her nipple, and then drawing it between his lips so he could work it against the roof of his mouth. He sucked on her until incoherent sobs were fighting their way through her parted lips and she was dripping down the insides of her trembling thighs.

His mouth found hers again and her hunger swiftly burst forth, despite the strange feeling of exposure and vulnerability. This time she kissed him back, her tongue every bit as wild and untamed as his own, eager to claim more of his heady taste. Their bodies went slick with heat and sweat, their mingled breaths choppy and raw.

That was it. The first soft stroke of her tongue and Ryan knew with a sickening certainty that he wasn't going to be able to stop with just this one taste of her. Not that he honestly wanted to do any such thing, but the rational part of his mind had still known it was wrong to take things this far.

Before she knew what he was doing, he dipped his finger into her pussy again—not deep, just enough to collect her cream—and then he lifted that finger up to his face and sucked the gleaming digit straight into his mouth. Shea watched in fascinated need as he licked it clean, his eyes burning with hunger while he held her stare. His hand was so wet with her juices that his lips were left glistening with them, the scent of her pussy sweet and clean as it filled the air between them, and she took in huge mouthfuls as she struggled for breath. Then his tongue flicked out to lick his lips, clearly savoring her taste, and she trembled as if he'd actually licked her own skin instead.

Ryan growled a dark, deep guttural sound that rumbled straight up from his chest. Watching her every moment of the way, he slowly lowered his face to hers. "Open your mouth," he grunted, and the second she parted her lips, he stroked them with his tongue. She groaned at the eroticism of the action, and then he sent his tongue deep, sharing her flavor with her in the sexiest way she could've ever imagined. Her heart beat so strong it felt like death, and yet her body had never felt more alive, as if every cell were crying out in need for this searing physical connection.

When he finally lifted his head, she was dazed and panting, her cheeks flushed with violent color. Ryan thought she looked like the most beautiful creature he'd ever seen. *And she was finally going to be his.*

He smiled down at her, his look far more dangerous than any she'd ever seen before, like that of a predator preparing to devour its next meal—as if he'd get under her skin, straight to the insatiable cravings buried beneath flesh and bone. When he spoke, his lust-roughened voice stroked her naked skin like a warm rush of pleasure, making her lower body clench, her pussy spasming in need, desperate for something to fill it. His fingers or tongue or cock! God, anything, she wanted to scream, *just get it in me!*

"You taste exactly how I knew you would, Shea. Your mouth, your cunt, your tits. Everything about you is just so damn sweet," he growled, leaning back enough to give him a clear view of her naked, quivering body. "You're just so damn beautiful—I can't stop looking at you," he grunted. "*Every incredible inch of this sweet little body—I just wanna fucking fill up on it!*"

In a thick, sensual haze, Shea watched him drop to his knees in front of her, felt his big hands on the insides of her trembling thighs, spreading them wide, forcing them to part for his shoulders. The width made her lose her balance, but he pressed into her, securing her legs, his face practically buried in her muff. *Jesus.* Was it just ten minutes ago that he'd never even touched her, not even a friggin' handshake, and now he was getting an up-close and personal shot of her dripping pussy, his nose nearly touching the small triangle of curls?

Ryan took a deep breath, flicking a quick glance up at her flushed, excited face. *Oh, yeah.* She wanted this as bad as he did. His fingers sifted through her delicate curls, teasing her, and he couldn't resist the temptation to watch as his long fingers tweaked through the silky little patch glistening with her juices. The lips of her cunt were preciously bare beneath her pretty black swirls of hair. "I love your little patch, Shea. It's soft, sexy as hell. And these bare lips, so slippery and wet, are just begging to be sucked and licked."

His fingers moved lower, skimming over her ripe, near-to-bursting clit, and he laughed a wicked sound of triumph when her body jolted in reaction. Then he moved the hand that had been gripping her thigh and used it to separate her pink, swollen lips, opening her cunt to him so he could take a nice long look. Damn it, he'd have liked more light, but wasn't willing to get up and go turn on another lamp.

Her belly hollowed out with her swift intake of breath, her thighs trembling with tension. "*Oh shit.*"

Ryan smiled at the tremor in her voice. "Mmm...I can see all of you now, Shea. Every soft, pink inch of your pretty cunt. It's gorgeous, baby. Fucking incredible." His fingers stroked over her, circling the tiny hole, and then, without warning, he shoved those two big, rough fingers straight up into her again, jerking a low scream from her throat.

Jesus, it was gonna damn near kill him when he finally got around to putting his cock in her. She was stretched tight around him, her inner muscles squeezing and contracting as they tried to make room for the thick intrusion.

Every muscle in his arm was tight and delineated as he slowly pulled his fingers free, and then he thrust again, shoving them deeper than before, and she clamped down on him so tightly this time that his breath hissed out between his teeth. "Keep your eyes on me," he growled. Then he leaned forward, flicked his tongue out against her swollen clit, pulled his fingers free, and shoved in three.

A strangled cry broke from her throat, but she managed to keep her big gray eyes on his, staring down at him over the pale, smooth skin of her stomach, the silver hoop in her navel glinting in the soft light, while her short nails dug into his naked shoulders.

One hand held her open, his other pulling out from between her legs to clutch tightly against her hip, his fingers biting hard enough to bruise. His head went lower, and he gave her one long, delicious lick that started at her vulva and ended in the soft stroking of his tongue across her clit again. And still she managed to hold his dark-eyed stare. Then he drew the throbbing, swollen knot of her clit into his mouth, nibbled with his teeth, gave it a gentle suck, and her mind fractured, thoughts spiraling out of control.

"*Damn...shit...oh damn it,*" she gasped, panting, and the sound of her desperation sent him right over the edge. With a deep, feral growl, his eyes closed and his mouth opened completely over her drenched cunt, taking all of it. His fingers had slipped away only to be replaced by the rough stab of his tongue as his face pressed into her, going deep as if he would crawl right up inside.

He kept her spread wide, his fingers hard, his body shuddering from the sight and smell and taste of her. All his senses were in complete, utter, catastrophic breakdown—a meltdown into total oblivion. The tiny mouth of her cunt nestled in that soft, pussy-pink flesh was quivering, gasping for him, as rivulets of pearly, syrupy sweet juice began streaming from the tiny slit.

Fuck. How in the hell was he ever going to fit in there? He'd rip her or tear her, when he'd rather die than cause her pain—but then, he'd die if he didn't get inside of her too. Shit, this was a nightmare and a friggin' fantasy fuck all rolled into one. He felt so raw, stripped of skin and muscle until there was nothing but this aching need for her that speared straight into his bones. His breathing came so hard and fast, he couldn't hear anything but his own violent whoosh of air; knew he wouldn't hear her if she begged him to stop, and still he held her open, pressed wide, exposed and vulnerable and his to do with as he pleased.

So utterly…undeniably *his*.

"Do you have any idea what I want to do to you? How bad I want to fuck you? How much I want to cram myself into this sweet little cunt, packing it full until you've taken every damn inch of me? Do you, Shea?"

His answer came in a low, keening sound of need that ripped from her throat, and before him, just a fraction from his mouth, her cunt gushed with cream until the satiny juices were gleaming down the insides of her pale thighs, dripping back into the little valley between the rosy cheeks of her beautiful ass.

Oh, fuck it, he couldn't take this. Before he could remember any of the things he knew about finesse and seduction and sex, his mouth was covering her again, his tongue shoved deep, spearing into that sweet hole, tongue-fucking her as if his very life depended on it. And damn it, maybe it did.

He was locked into her, ready to eat his way through, his mouth and tongue sucking and stroking, drinking her down his throat like fine wine. For the first time in his life, Ryan was locked into a woman's pussy, not because of ego or sense of fair play, but because he'd go mad if he didn't have her taste in his head. He wasn't breathing now, wasn't sure if his heart was even still beating, but he was eating her as if he couldn't live without the taste of her in his mouth, drawing sustenance from this grasping slit.

His face pressed into her, his throat working, and he pushed up harder against her slippery flesh. Closer — hell, he had to get closer. His head angled for a tighter fit. His fingers bit into the soft swell of her ass, holding her up, angling her so he could get even deeper, and…oh, God, he was there…just drinking her in…his tongue hitting the perfect spot over and over and over. She closed around him, milking his tongue, pulling it into her convulsing sheath, and he pressed harder, his entire face buried in the sweet humid warmth of her cunt.

Now he could hear her raw, screaming cries of release over the roaring in his ears. She came long and hard and heavy, flooding against his face, into his mouth, and he just kept going. He couldn't stop. It'd taken him over, like some primal, primitive force trying to draw him into this woman forever. He felt like a drowning man who'd surrendered himself to the currents. Hell, he didn't know if he'd ever be able to pull his tongue out of her without dying to shove it right back up this hot little cunt. He'd never be able to look at her and not remember her taste, not think about doing this again and again. Never think about her and not want to go down on her more than he wanted his next breath.

Oh, shit. He had to get the fuck away from her! Now!

Shea trembled against the wall as he quickly pulled back, stumbling to his feet a safe distance away from her naked, gleaming body that was wildly flushed and so obviously ready. His head was spinning and he knew the look in his eyes was wild, his features drawn tight in a hard scowl, which she'd see as soon as she managed to open her eyes.

The tiny spasms of pleasure that remained shuddered through her body, quivering through her muscles, flowing through her blood. *Okay*, she thought. *Mmm...wow*. That was *sooo* not what she'd expected. His tongue—so soft, yet rough—gentle, yet hard. A small smile broke across her face with the thought that if fucking him was as good as this had been, then she was setting herself up for a really big addiction. The pleasure pumping through her was definitely a narcotic, and she had the uncomfortable feeling that it was going to be more than painful if her plans failed here tonight and he walked away from her.

She filled her lungs with a much-needed gulp of air, knowing she'd avoided looking at him long enough. She opened her heavy lids, surprised, not to mention severely disappointed by the look in the dark blue eyes staring back at her. *Well, hell.* She may have limited experience when it came to these things, but she was fairly positive that the look on his face was not a good sign.

There was just a flash of a moment that she thought she was going to cry, just break down and bawl like a friggin' baby after the events of the night, but she pulled it together in time, pleased to find that she had more backbone than that. She used it to hide the frustration in her as best she could, knowing on some weird, instinctual female level that he'd pulled away from her in more than just the physical sense. No, she wasn't going to get her chance after all, and to be honest, she'd rather go without than have him take her with that strange look on his face, as if he didn't know whether he wanted to kiss her or kill her.

Some dignity would be good at a time like this, not to mention some clothes, but she thought it'd look too ridiculous to go bending down for her dress at this point. Whatever chance at modesty she'd had was long gone by now, so she straightened her shoulders and tried for as much bravado as she could muster. Then found she could muster pretty well.

"Well, I'll, um, just say thanks I guess and go get my shower. If it's not too much trouble, lock up on your way out."

Praying her legs wouldn't give out and land her flat on her face, she walked to the bathroom, still wearing her silly sandals. She didn't take another breath until the door was safely locked behind her. Without listening for the sounds of him leaving, Shea turned on the shower, stepped beneath the hot spray, and washed the evidence of the last fifteen minutes away as best she could.

Too bad she had a feeling the memories were going to last a lifetime.

Chapter Four

Fuck. Ryan couldn't believe he'd panicked and just let her walk away! What the hell was the matter with him?

Shit, he'd never had his two heads cause such a big friggin' problem in his entire life. Thinking and sex did not go together, end of story. So then why did she have him so twisted up in knots he couldn't keep even that simple fact straight? Damn woman had him going out of his mind!

Now she was in the shower, after delivering her cool dismissal, while he stood rooted in place, his cock about ready to climb up his body and strangle him for screwing this up—and his mind still reeling from the emotional assault she'd made on him.

He needed to get it together before she came back out, because no way in hell was he leaving her alone. He might be scared shitless of the way she made him feel, all desperate and needy and like a keg of dynamite just waiting to blow, but he wasn't such a prick that he was going to leave her by herself tonight.

And if his dick was snickering, knowing his motivation was a hell of a lot more than honorable, he did his best to ignore it. He may have screwed up his chance to fuck her tonight, but Ryan knew they weren't done. Not by a long shot. He just had to figure out how to get inside of her without doing something really stupid and falling—

No!

No. Fucking. Way!

Damn it, he wasn't even going to think it.

Needing a quick distraction, Ryan searched out his discarded shirt, slipped it over his head, and began the stubborn task of trying to hide his cock behind his fly again. After some careful maneuvering, he finally got the damn thing put away, but no way in hell was it hidden, leaving a long, highly noticeable ridge from the base of his zipper all the way over to his left hip. But, at least it was no longer poking its head out, begging for attention.

That taken care of, Ryan collected the shattered pieces of the lamp she'd crashed over Spalding's skull, dumping them in her kitchen rubbish bin. Then he figured he might as well take the opportunity to get to learn more about the woman turning his entire world upside down, and since the water was still running, he started a slow walk around her bedroom.

For a guy with really rugged taste, he was kinda surprised how much he liked it. It was feminine, but not frilly, with books crammed into every available space and thick, scented candles decorating every surface. A case packed full of CDs caught his eye on the other side of the room, standing next to her dresser which had her sound system on top, and he walked over for a quick look, interested to know what kind of music she was into.

His eyes scanned the titles, and he snorted. Huh—it figured. There were rows and rows of alternative rock, along with countless classical compilations and operas, for crying out loud. But then he finally found some Stones, and Pink Floyd, and The Who, so maybe there was hope after all. She didn't have any Springsteen or Clapton, but hey, he could always remedy that later on.

And whoa—what in the hell was he talking about now? Where did this shit keep coming from? Jesus, it wasn't like they were getting ready to play house or anything. He just wanted to fuck her, not move in with her!

The water was still running, and he was quickly looking for another distraction when her phone rang. Not thinking twice about it, Ryan walked over to her bedside table and lifted the receiver, muttering, "McCall," into the mouthpiece.

"Uh...Ry? Is that you?"

Well, shit.

"Yeah, Hannah, it's me. What's up?" he drawled offhandedly, suddenly realizing his mouth was still wet from going down on Shea. He wiped his face against his shoulder, trying to ignore the very un-ignorable taste of her cunt in his mouth, coating his tongue like sweet, addictive syrup.

Damn it, why hadn't he kept his stupid shit together and nailed her while he had the chance? If screwing her was half as good as eating her, it was something he definitely didn't want to miss, no matter how uneasy she made him.

Shit, he grumbled to himself, realizing Hannah was talking into his ear and he hadn't even been listening. "Damn it, Ryan, are you—I mean, you are at Shea's place, right? My Shea—as in my best friend?"

"Hmm. Seems that way," he replied silkily, suddenly angry with Hannah for telling Shea about Red's. Not that he wasn't happy with the consequences now, considering he was still reeling from her flavor, but Shea could've been seriously hurt because of their scheming—and to top it off, he didn't care for the tone of Hannah's voice. "Shea's in the shower and I'm just waiting for her to get out. You got a problem with any of that, Hannah?"

His oldest friend laughed her husky, throaty laugh on the other end of the line. "Uh, no need to sound so surly, Ry. I've been trying to get you two together for months now. I just, ah, hope you know what you're doing. I mean—Shea's not the kind of woman you play around with." And despite her sweet tone, there was a wealth of warning in her words, reminding him of that mean streak she'd had before her ex-husband got his hands on her.

He was almost happy to see its return—just not at this particular moment in time. Refusing to let her put him on the defensive, he clipped, "You mean she's not like the usual women I pick up at Red Mackey's place?"

Ryan could almost hear her grimace over the connection. "Oh God, she really went there tonight, didn't she? What happened? Is she okay? Damn it, I told her to wait until I got back."

Instead of answering her string of questions, Ryan asked one of his own while pacing the length of the bedroom. "What the hell were you thinking, sending her to a place like that?"

"It's not like I had planned for her to go by herself. I was going to make her take me along as backup."

"Yeah, well, you weren't there, and neither was I," he muttered angrily, the terror he'd felt when he'd heard Shea's muffled screams twisting him into knots all over again. "But the bastard who broke into her apartment tonight sure as hell was."

"Oh shit," she gasped, voice hollow with fear. "Tell me she's okay, Ry. I knew something was wrong. I knew it! That's why I'm calling so late. I went to bed early tonight, but I woke up with the worst feeling a moment ago and had to call."

"Derek and I took care of the asshole before he was able to do much more than scare the hell out of her." And damn it, his hands were suddenly shaking just thinking of the few strikes Spalding had gotten in.

Ryan wanted to go down to the station and knock him on his drunken ass all over again. Shit, what he really wanted was to beat the guy to a bloody pulp for laying his filthy hands on *his woman*, and it had him burning with anger that he wasn't going to be able to do just that. He should've kicked the crap outta the bastard when he'd had the chance.

Hannah's voice brought him back to the conversation. "And so you're spending the night with her? You're going to stay there with her?" They both knew that what she was really saying was *you're going to sleep with her.*

"You know, as much as I love you, Hannah, I don't think that's any of your business."

There was silence for a moment, and then she said, "Shea's my best friend, Ry. She's also not half as jaded as you and so yes, that makes it my business. I don't want her getting hurt if you're not willing to offer her more than a quick fuck. She deserves more than that and you know it."

"Just be glad I'm happy with your scheming tonight," Ryan drawled, looking to sway the focus away from his plans for Shea and his own uneasiness about them, to Hannah and Derek, "or I might be tempted to stick my nose in your own sex life and lend old Kiely a hand with you."

She groaned, but ignored the loaded comment, saying instead, "Fine, I'm going to go now, but I'll call back on

Sunday before I head home. I'd call tomorrow, but I'm going to be visiting my grandmother in the hospital all day."

"Fine. I'll tell Shea you called and that you'll call on Sunday."

More silence, and then, "Okay. But remember what I said, Ry. Hurt her and I'm going to make you sorry. I'll become the biggest pain in the butt you've ever known. It'll be worse than that time I put fire ants in your bed after you stole my bra and sold it to that snake Peter Gaze in the sixth grade. Godzilla will be like a teddy bear compared to me. You know I love you, Ry, but somebody's got to keep you in line. Got it?"

The water was off now, and suddenly all he could think about was Shea's wet, warm, dripping body—his for the taking. He gritted his teeth and muttered, "Yeah. Later, Hannah. And I love you too."

He hung up the phone, sprawled out on the bed, and tried not to think about how badly he wanted to sink inside of the woman about to walk through the bathroom door. Knowing he needed a distraction, he unclipped his cell phone from his belt and called in to check his voicemail at work.

While he went through his messages, a paperback caught his attention on her bedside table. Without really thinking about it, just acting on his natural curiosity where this woman was concerned, he reached out and grabbed it, flicking through the pages with his thumb until he randomly stopped about midway through.

The first word he saw caught his attention, but the second one nearly made his eyes bug out.

Holy shit! Who would've ever thought it? Scholarly little Shea liked to read women's erotica. How freaking stunning was that? He'd have smiled at the thought of her lying in this bed, snuggled up with her book and sexy little story…if only the thought didn't make him fucking hard as nails.

What did she do when she read this stuff? Did she get wet? Did she reach between her sweet, slender thighs and stroke her clit? Finger her pussy? His eyes squeezed shut while a painful torrent of erotic images burned through his brain, leaving him shaky and aching and damn near on the verge of ripping out his cock and pumping himself to some sort of peace right there and then.

No matter how well he thought he had this woman pegged, she kept shifting the tables on him. Going to Red's to try and pick him up. Wearing that little fuck-me dress and sandals, looking like a wet dream on legs. Reading soft-core erotica that would have made even the women at Red's blush. Jesus, no wonder he was so damn fascinated with her.

Five minutes later, Ryan was still halfway listening to the sound of Derek's voice giving him an update on Spalding, while his twisted imagination tortured him with image upon image of Shea. He saw her spread-eagled on her bed, knees up, the graceful fingers of one hand holding the lips of her cunt wide while the fingers of the other stroked and dipped into that sweet little hole that his tongue had been shoved up not fifteen minutes ago.

Oh Christ. He was trembling, a trickle of sweat dripping across his brow at the jaw-grinding visual assault, when she finally came through the door, flushed and smelling sweetly of vanilla, reminding him that he hadn't eaten.

Well, food at least.

"You took long enough," he muttered, his tone rougher than he'd intended. His eyes devoured her near-naked body while Derek's voice became a nondescript noise in the background, his complete attention captured by Shea.

She nearly lost her hold on her towel as she jumped a foot in the air at the husky sound of his voice. "You scared the hell out of me!" she yelped, spinning around to pin him with a glare, careful to keep the slipping towel in place. "What are you still doing here?"

He flashed a hungry smile, holding up the book she'd last laid on her bedside table.

Oh crap.

Not *that* one.

It wasn't that she was embarrassed by her reading choices. No, she was woman enough to know that there was nothing wrong with indulging her sexual fantasies with the help of some well-written erotica. Nonetheless, there was something decidedly awkward about being caught in nothing but a towel, while her dream man—who had just given her head—lay there on her bed as if he were a pasha waiting for her to come and grant his sexual wishes. Desire and lust hit her hard and high, and her pussy flooded while her face and breasts flushed a deep, aroused shade of red.

Ryan's smile widened. "Interesting reading, honey. I never would've pegged you as a 'cock' and 'cunt' kind of girl, but I gotta admit I like it. I guess there are all kinds of fun things we get to learn about each other, huh?"

She stared at him in utter frustration, torn between making a cutting comment about his snooping habits and shamelessly throwing herself at him, begging him to take her every which way he could, twenty times this side of Sunday. No—damn it, she had more pride than that! But it wasn't easy to hold back, especially with him propped up on her pillows, his muscles bulging beneath his T-shirt and jeans in *all* the right places. And she really, really wanted to get her hands on that beautiful cock of his again.

Oh, man…the things she would do with it if given half a chance. The thought was almost too tempting for her self-control, so she padded on bare feet to her dresser, determined to ignore the long, sexy body draped across her bed, apparently once again listening to someone on his cell phone. She grabbed her favorite pair of jammies and went back into the bathroom to change, thankful that he'd at least put his shirt back on and refastened his fly. The less of that magnificent, muscle-honed flesh she saw, the better—that is, if she was expected not to jump and drool all over it.

And despite the fact that he'd been a total jerk, a part of her couldn't help but love the sight of him in *her* bed. It was strange how he looked like he belonged there. While she'd brushed her teeth, she'd wondered how many times she'd lain in that bed and listened to him screwing some other woman through the connecting bedroom wall of their apartments. Since she'd moved in, how many nights had she gone to switch off her CD player with one hand while crossing the fingers of her other, praying that she wasn't going to be treated to yet another resounding performance of *ooh-ahh-mmm, bang-bang-bang*?

It'd been over a week since the last time she'd been awakened by his wall-thumping entertainment, and she was still hearing the disturbing noises in her sleep. Disturbing because of the way they affected her.

Disturbing because she'd never in her life really believed a man could make a woman utter the kind of carnal sounds that no amount of drywall could contain. Disturbing because she *wanted*, more than anything in the world, to be the woman making those *oohs* and *ahhs* and *mmms* — all of which led up to the most erotic, raw sounding cries she had ever imagined.

Of course, she'd done a fair bit of screaming tonight herself, she mused, applying a thin layer of lightly scented moisturizer to her freshly scrubbed face. She almost smiled at the thought of how she'd wailed like a banshee when he'd finally pushed her over the edge with that wicked tongue of his and she'd come all over him. Knowing her cheeks were probably crimson at the delicious memory, she carefully avoided looking in the mirror while she went about the rest of her nightly routine, rubbing moisturizer into her skin and attempting to detangle the riot of black curls she called hair.

She didn't want to face her ridiculous embarrassment, and she really didn't want to be reminded of all the differences between her and the women who usually caught Ryan McCall's eye. They always tended to be tall, where she was not, and tended to be on the somewhat top-heavy side of things, which she could only dream about. And, like the gorgeous stud, they took a casual attitude toward sex that she simply couldn't comprehend. Hell, it wasn't that she judged it, she just couldn't get her head around how something so personal could be approached with so little meaning.

Then again, she was one to talk. Look at her and Jimmy Prescott. When she'd begun to agonize over the fact that she was the only admitted virgin left in her acquaintance, she'd slept with Jimmy — given her virginity to the jerk—when she really didn't know him at all. Geez, as if the night weren't already screwed up enough as it was, she had to go and think about that nightmare. Could this get any crappier?

When she came back out and Ryan was still there, minus the phone now, she paused in the doorway, crossed her arms, and said, "Why are you still here?"

Lounging back on her pillows, one leg lying atop her bed while the other hung off the side, foot on the floor and knee swinging, he looked like an ad for why good girls should always take at least one turn being bad. Shea licked her lips and tried real hard not to do that drooling thing, while reminding herself that, though she liked the thought of playing the wicked little sex kitten, she obviously didn't do it very well.

Otherwise, she'd be having fun getting dirty, instead of having just gotten clean.

Everything about the man made her think of hot, sweaty, mind-shattering sex. There was just something about his sinful looks and the way he held himself, the constant blaze of heat firing his gaze, which reduced her to a quivering, pulsing mass of need every damn time she set eyes on him.

He lay there against her pillows, looking good enough to eat—and she'd have loved the chance to get that huge, hard, hot cock of his in her mouth for a long, lingering taste. His strong jaw was covered with the beginnings of sexy stubble, and she'd have loved to run her tongue along there as well, until she reached his ear and could taunt the sensitive hollow with her teasing breath. She wanted to run her tongue over his silky skin, savoring his rich, earthy flavor, filling her head with his warm, erotic scent. Actually, she'd have liked the chance to taste and breathe in every inch of him, from the top of his tawny head down to his two big feet.

The muted light from her lamp played across his rugged features and golden scrub of hair, the short strands rakishly disheveled from where he continually ran his hands through them. At the moment, one hand rested on his hard abdomen, fingers idly stroking, making her wish they were her own, the other propped behind his head, causing the hard muscles in his arm to bulge, stretching the seams of his T-shirt.

It seemed that everywhere she looked, he bulged with long, lean muscles, his body a mesmerizing work of art in the soft light and shadows. What would it feel like to be at the mercy of all that magnificent power and strength? To feel the delicious weight of his body against her own, those hard muscles pressing her down, holding her at his mercy as he pounded into her, losing control and giving her everything he could? His powerful physique intoxicated her with its masculine beauty, and the bastard knew it. His high cheekbones were hot with the flush of arousal, and the telling expression on his handsome face said he was only too aware of how he affected her, the cocky lift at the corner of his silky lips a testament to his arrogance.

God, he wasn't even doing anything, was just lying there, for crying out loud, and she still couldn't tear her eyes away. Everything about him was a seduction and a sin, from the thick ridge of his cock beneath the worn denim of his jeans, to the look in his eyes that once again said he wanted to take her hard and rough and deep.

He scooted down, making himself more comfortable, his blue eyes traveling over her, the heated look in them telling her he wasn't going anywhere anytime soon. It also said he liked what he saw.

Well, at least that much had changed, she thought with a wry groan. He no longer looked right through her, but seemed to take notice of the fact she was a woman. The knowledge of just how much evidence he had of that fact made her want to start blushing again, but she managed to fight back the telling action and repeated her question. "Why are you still here, Ry?"

Instead of answering her, he smiled and said, "You sure as hell took enough time to clean up." He hated the unfamiliar thread of need in his voice, but there was no help for it. Just looking at her made his pulse race—his heart pump like a son-of-a-bitch. Damn it, he *was* needy, because he sure as hell needed her, and that should have had him running like hell, instead of planting his ass in her bed as if he never planned on getting back out of it. "You know, you can scrub all you want, Shea—but I don't wash away that easily."

"Thanks for the warning," she drawled too sweetly, clearly still pissed with him. "I'll be sure to keep that in mind."

His stomach growled at him, reminding him he was hungry, but she didn't look as if she were going to offer up the use of her kitchen for a midnight snack. A midnight fuck would be even better, but he didn't think that was going to be an option either. He'd pissed her off, but good, with his weird little moment of panic back there, and she sure as hell didn't look like she was in the mood to be forgiving. Not that he could blame her.

Christ, she'd had one hell of a night, and he sure as shit hadn't helped the situation.

And he couldn't help but smile at her spunk, finding her too adorable for words standing there in her threadbare shorts and shirt, glaring at him as if he were a bug she was getting ready to squash. "Hannah called while you were in the shower. Said she'd call back on Sunday."

Shea's answering smile felt tight, as if her face might crack with tension any second now. "Great. Thanks for the message. Now you can *go*."

"I'm not leaving you alone after you were physically assaulted, nearly raped, and have a front door that's busted open." His posture was casual, completely belying the hard-edged tone of his voice.

Well, when he put it like that, maybe she really didn't want to be alone tonight after all. She was, however, going to sleep alone. "Fine then, but you sleep on the couch."

He glanced at his watch, and then leveled another heated look on her, one she felt all the way to her toes. "It's still early for me—for a Friday night," he replied casually, as if they found themselves in this exact, bizarre situation all the time.

"Yeah, well, it's late for me, Ry."

For a split second he looked as if he'd argue, but then his eyes found the bruise on her cheek and he apparently changed his mind. Rolling off the bed, he grabbed the throw she had folded across the bottom. When he reached her side, he tilted her chin toward him with the edge of his fist, waiting for her questioning gaze to meet his steady blue one. "I'll be out here if you need me."

Shea blinked, trying to hide the fact that she did—but he was already gone.

Chapter Five

The first thing Ryan realized when he opened his eyes to the early morning sunlight streaming through the slanted blinds was that he wasn't on the couch.

The second was that he was in her bed.

Shea's bed.

Holy fucking shit! He took two deep breaths while he struggled to ignore the feel of her all but wrapped around him, and searched for the memory that explained why his ass wasn't where he'd planted it last night...after eating her out...and then being a total ass and pissing her off.

It took him a few moments, but he finally got it. He'd awakened sometime around three to the sound of Shea crying out in her sleep, and like the pathetic idiot he was, he'd come in here to make sure she was okay and ended up holding her until she fell asleep again. Only he'd obviously fallen asleep too, and now look at him.

He had two really bad friggin' problems here, the first being that the intoxicating woman whose bed he was in was all but tied in a knot with him. The second was even worse because it meant that it was about damn time he faced up to the truth and stopped lying to himself.

Despite his reservations, and the complications he knew it would cause, he was more than ready to physically involve himself with the delectable Shea Dresden in every possible way there was, no matter how much shit it landed him in. There was no physical domain on that gorgeous body of hers that he didn't long to dominate and control, explore and exploit.

If the size and stiffness of his morning wood was any indication, he was in some serious fucking trouble here. The fact that she was resting one hand low on his abs, just to the right of his raging hard-on, definitely didn't help the situation. And the fact that one of his own hands had wedged itself snugly between her soft, slender thighs, while his other arm wrapped tightly around her shoulders, cradling her face against his chest, was even worse.

Hell, he'd slept with scores of women, but it'd never felt like this. Usually waking up in a woman's bed made him edgy, tense, and eager for escape. It *did not* make him want to hold her closer and fall back asleep with her in his arms, or better yet, wake her up with a soft, sleepy morning ride. Why was Shea so damn different? Why did she fit against him as if it were exactly where she belonged? And why was he worrying about a way to convince her to let him stay instead of doing the usual and getting the hell out of there?

With each breath she drew in, her soft breasts crushed against his ribcage, and the exquisite torture was quickly triggering a painful throbbing right in the core of his cock. The urge to press his hand higher between her thighs, until his fingers were investigating her sweet, sleep-soft cunt had him groaning aloud.

The deep rumble echoed through his chest, and Ryan watched through heavy-lidded eyes as Shea softly began to stir. She stretched lazily, like a well-rested kitten, making him smile. To his immense relief and utter frustration, it moved her down in the bed, until his hand nestled right against the heated juncture of her thighs.

Oh hell.

He could feel the warmth of her cunt through the thin barrier of her jersey shorts, the same cunt he'd had his face shoved into just about seven hours ago, and his body shuddered in reaction. His fingers flexed, moving against the swollen cleft, and he knew she hadn't bothered to wear panties beneath the soft material. Christ, just a shred of insubstantial cotton and he'd be touching warm, wet pussy. His nostrils flared, sweat broke out across his brow, and his jaw locked. He struggled to keep his fingers still, when all he really wanted was to push the crotch of her shorts aside and feel her against his skin.

It was a jaw-grinding, physical ache not to press between them, to seek out her pulsing, swollen clit and stroke her until she came like a warm flood against his hand. Screwing his eyes shut, he imagined sinking his finger deep into that narrow slit again, feeling it squeeze him so tight. Then he'd sink in another, tongue her nipples until she relaxed around him, and force her to take three, stretching her until there was a chance in hell he'd be able to work his cock up into her. Then he'd plow hard and deep until his balls were jammed up against her ass and his cock-head was nudging the back of her throat.

Ryan felt his balls tighten, the first few drops of cum seeping from his slit, and realized with a muffled curse that he was about to explode just from thinking about fucking her. He groaned, feeling like a thirteen-year-old boy waking up in the tumultuous throes of a wrenchingly wicked wet dream. He wanted to laugh and swear and bang his head against the blasted wall all at the same time.

And he really wanted to screw the brains out of the pretty little imp lying in his arms.

Her eyelids flickered with movement, a rapid beat of long lashes against creamy skin, and then she was looking up at him, her gaze cloudy and unfocused from sleep. There were lines of uncertainty between her finely arched brows, but sensual interest beginning to burn bright in her eyes. "What are you doing?" she asked in a husky murmur.

"Nothing at the moment," he drawled. "If you want to keep it that way, I suggest you move your hand."

Shea smiled, looking like the cat that'd just swallowed the canary, feathers and all. "Yeah? Where do you think I should move it?"

He gave up the fight and nudged his cock into her, hitting her hip, letting her feel how massive she'd made him. "Hell, it really must've been too long for you if you can't figure that one out on your own, sugar."

Shea stared up at him, awed by the smoldering blue of his heavy-lidded gaze and the strong jaw covered in dark golden stubble, both of which took his already irresistible good looks to the point of overkill. He was just so damn sexy—it was hell on a girl's resolve not to fall all over him.

His hand moved against her, his thumb sliding beneath the edge of her shorts, stroking the naked lips of her pussy as they grew slicker and slicker for him. Her breath caught on a sharp gasp and he smiled. "You really do need to be fucked, don't you?"

Not by just anyone, she thought with a delicious shiver. *Only by you.*

But she was going to be damned before she let him screw her for the sake of charity, like it was his duty as a guy to make sure she got her sex fix. *Men*, she screamed inside her head, rolling out of the bed before he could grab hold of her.

"I'm not interested in a pity fuck, Ry. So thanks—but no thanks. I guess I'll just keep waiting until I find a man who wants me as much as I want him."

"Like hell you will," he snarled, rolling out of the bed, his boxers tenting high and hard in front of him, drawing her eyes against her will.

She tried to look away, but Jesus—what woman in her right mind wouldn't stare at that thing when it was being so brilliantly displayed?

Shea just kept staring while he stood there, fighting an internal struggle she knew nothing about, but as soon as he started around the end of the bed, straight toward her, she started backing up. Back, back, back, until she came up hard against the wall in the same damn place she'd been last night when he'd gone down on her. When he'd showed her that whatever measly pleasure she'd managed to give herself over the years was nothing compared to what Ryan McCall could deliver.

Knowing the question was as asinine as it sounded, she asked it anyway. "What do you think you're doing?"

"You offered me a fuck last night," he rasped, the husky sound scraping delicately across her skin, leaving chills in its wake. "Now I'm taking you up on it."

Shea lifted her chin, trying to ignore the rush of heat flooding between her legs, readying her body for his, softening her cunt for the thick penetration of that massive cock in his shorts. "In case you haven't noticed, Ry, I changed my mind. You're being an ass and I'd rather screw a snake."

Shit, he knew he was being an ass, but what other option did he have? There was too much at stake here—*too much of him at risk* — and this dick-of-the-year attitude was his last shred of defense between sanity and falling headfirst into an emotional unknown that he feared as much as he craved. An unknown that had him completely at this woman's mercy, his heart hers to do with as she pleased, until she finally told him to fuck off and get lost. And then where would he be?

Uh-uh...no way, he growled, but his body wasn't listening. It just kept moving in on her, ready to take everything it had wanted and had been denied for too damn long.

He reached her right on the ending consonant, grabbing her wrists and jerking them above her head in a thrilling action of control that excited her more than she could comfortably admit. But damn, it was hard to stay angry when his big, beautiful, half-naked body was pressing into her, making it blatantly obvious he could crush her if he wanted — not to mention anything else that came to mind.

"A snake, huh? Well, that's too damn bad, Shea, because you're going to be screwing *me*."

She knew it was useless, but she struggled against the restraint of her wrists, her wriggling body only making his that much harder, and had her baby doll tee rising up her torso in the process. "Nice try, Ry, but I know you'd never force me."

His smile was slow and sweet and sexy. "Who said anything about forcing you, sugar? By the time I'm done with you, you're gonna be beggin' for it."

She bucked with all her strength, but he didn't budge. "Oh, get off of me, you ass! I may want to fuck you, Ry, but not when you're being a jerk!"

"Yeah, well, beggars can't be choosers, sweetheart."

Her eyes flashed with equal parts fury and hunger, as hot and violent as lightning. "Fuck you."

He winced on the inside, knowing he deserved that one, but was nowhere near being able to control the stream of crap pouring out of his mouth. His defenses had fallen into instinctual battle mode, ready to do or say whatever it took to keep this woman at a distance, while all his body could think about was getting into her. As deep into her as he could go. His heart wanted the same damn thing, and that was the bitch of the situation right there. The more his body and heart wanted her—hungered for her with every fiber and facet of his being—the harder his defenses struggled against it.

He leaned down and licked the side of her neck, just beneath her ear. "Do I hear a pretty please?"

Her mouth opened, but whatever cutting comeback she'd had ready to hurl back in his face got swallowed down his throat instead. It was an instant possession, so thorough she could barely breathe, but then air suddenly didn't seem nearly as necessary as his tongue and taste and lips devouring her own.

Her head spun with every delicious stroke of his tongue, each deliberate nip of his teeth. There was no way to find herself in such a vicious rush of sensation, the raging pulse of pleasure throbbing within her, centered between her trembling legs. Then she felt her body braced up high against the wall, Ryan's hot hands slipping beneath her shorts to grip her naked bottom, his hips pushing insistently between her legs, spreading them to make room for him.

"*Fuck*," he growled, not knowing if it was a curse or an order and too hard to care. All that mattered was getting inside of her as soon as possible, and he couldn't even wait until they made it back over to the bed. He had to be crammed up into her fist-tight little cunt right then, that very second. Had to feel it milking him of every drop he had, releasing the agonizing pressure in his cum-filled balls.

Without hesitation, he pushed the waistband of his boxers down. Shoving the loose crotch of her shorts out of his way, his hand moved between her legs, two thick fingers digging deeply into her pussy, wringing a guttural cry from her lips, a sound she'd never imagined she could make. The rush of need was instantaneous, as if they'd been going hard and heavy at the foreplay for hours instead of only just rolling out of bed. And it was strong enough to force its way past the anger, transforming that volatile emotion into an even more powerful craving.

Who in the hell could stay pissed when they were about to be taken up against the wall by the sexiest, most desirable man they'd ever known? The one who'd invaded her heart and wasn't budging from the claim he'd made there?

Shea knew she sure as hell couldn't.

She felt his body tighten, his muscles going taut, and then her legs were caught over his strong forearms. His hands found her ass again, fingers biting into the delicate flesh as he pulled the soft globes apart, opening her even more. She jerked in his arms, completely at his mercy, and then the broad, blunt head of his cock was nudging against her drenched slit, pressing within. At the hot feel of his naked flesh, she froze in his arms, eyes shocked wide.

"Wh-what…" she gasped, trying to think over the roaring of her blood, "what about protection?"

Apparently, he'd forgotten about it, along with his claim to make her beg, and while she wasn't reminding him about the latter, she needed to address the former.

His defenses in shambles, destroyed by the necessity of having her right where he wanted her, Ryan barely held himself back from thrusting—the hot, wet feel of her cunt gripping the head of his dick nearly driving him over the edge. "You're not on the pill?" he demanded with a rough growl, unable to believe he was getting ready to pound into her without a rubber. Hell, if she hadn't stopped him, he'd already be buried deep without even having thought about it.

It was even more surprising to find that now that he had, he still didn't want to put one on. Fuck it. If he was going out on the edge to dance with the devil, then he wanted it all—wanted her flesh to flesh. Wanted to feel her against his naked cock, all that slippery wet heat grasping him so damn tight.

It was unthinkable.

It was insane.

But it was what he wanted. The fact that she could affect him in such a way—that she was the *only* woman who'd ever affected him like this—only made him that much more wary of her. He knew he should turn tail and run as far and fast as he could in the opposite direction, but they'd already gone too far. There was no turning back now. He was fucking helpless before her, at the mercy of everything he'd felt for her from the very beginning—

defenseless against those deeper wants and desires that had steadily stretched to life during these past weeks while he'd struggled to stay away from her.

Ryan waited forever for her answer, his muscles aching from holding back and sweat beading on his brow.

Finally, she whispered, "A doctor, uh, put me on the pill for regularity." Shea didn't think now was the time to tell Ryan she'd actually gone on it because she'd planned on seducing him. "But what about diseases?"

He stiffened in her arms. "I'm not going to give you anything, damn it!"

She refused to let him intimidate her, unable to believe they were still arguing, with him poised just inside her straining body. He felt huge there, and though it burned, she couldn't wait to feel all of that throbbing hardness buried deep inside of her very empty, very needy pussy. "Don't yell at me, Ryan. You told me yourself what you go to Red's for."

His eyes caught hers, holding her captive. "I haven't screwed without a rubber since I was eighteen, and old enough to know better," he told her in a low voice. "But how about you?" he asked just to taunt her, knowing she was the epitome of health and cleanliness. Everything about her was fresh and untouched, as if she really were as innocent as she looked.

Her face flamed hotter. "I won't give you anything, if that's what you're asking."

"Then this conversation's over, so let's—"

"Wait!"

Ryan's forehead dropped to hers, his dick screaming at him in protest to get on with it already, and fuck. "Christ, what now?"

"Why not with me?"

His head shot up like he'd been clipped on the chin. "Why not with you what?" he gritted through his clenched teeth, wondering if she was trying to torture him to death by making him hold back.

Shea hated stopping him, wanting him inside of her so badly, but she had to know if he'd just given her a clue as to how he felt. "Why not wear a—a condom with me," she panted, "when you said that's what you always do?"

Those beautiful blue eyes of his narrowed in frustration. Then he smiled—a slow, sexy smile full of carnal lust and hunger. "Because," he explained in a husky rasp, nipping at her mouth, her chin, "I don't want anything to stop me from feeling all this snug, slick heat when I do *this*." His muscles flexed and he pushed up into her, surprised when he couldn't go further than a few inches.

She clamped down on him, *hard*, her inner muscles fighting his penetration, her slender, delicate fingers digging into the bulging muscles of his biceps. He moved slowly until he realized only a hard lunge was going to force him past the unusually tight resistance of her body.

Shea moaned.

Ryan growled a beastly, guttural sound that felt as if it had surged straight up from the root of his cock.

She squirmed in his arms, forcing him a little deeper. Her mouth opened, but she couldn't draw in enough air to tell him what she needed—which was his body pounding into her, filling her up, hard and heavy and fast. Then she felt the tremor move through him.

"Open your eyes, Shea. Look at me!"

Her lids fluttered, her hungry gaze locked with his, and then he plowed up into her, going hard and straight and deep, driving his way through her clenching muscles with brutal force until he was fully seated inside of her, buried to the hilt.

Shea screamed from the strength of the blow, back arched against the wall, arms flung out at her sides. She felt impaled, deliciously filled, the sensation of having Ryan packed deep inside of her so much better than any fantasy she'd ever had. Everything was perfect, from the hot press of his hard body pushing her against the wall, to the even hotter, harder press of his fascinating erection rammed against her womb.

And then through the pulsing throb of pleasure, she realized he'd gone completely still. *Uh-oh.* She peeked at him from beneath her lashes and saw his head flung far back against his shoulders. He stared at the ceiling instead of her, his chest working like a great billowing sail between them.

Forcing her arms to move, Shea touched him lightly on his wide shoulders, then the strong column of his throat. "Ryan?" she asked breathlessly, unsure if he could hear her over the rushing of his breath. The harsh expression on his handsome face tightened at the sound of her voice, his body shuddered against her own, and then she was drowning in the deep blue depths of his eyes.

"Goddamn it, Shea," he groaned in an awful voice. The feel of her hot little pussy was so damn tight, he knew there was no way in hell she'd ever done this more than once or twice. *Jesus!* She was squeezing him so damn hard it felt like he was going to explode inside of her any second now, and he gritted his teeth to keep from losing it too soon. "You're practically a fucking *virgin* and you didn't tell me?" he accused, snarling it as if it were a dirty word. "*How could you not fucking tell me?*"

Her big eyes went completely round. "Would you have really cared? And I didn't think you'd be able—well, that you'd be able to tell. I mean—it's not like I *am* a virgin, Ry. I've had sex. I've had orgasms." Not all at the same time, of course, but he didn't need to know all her secrets. No way in hell was she admitting that she was the only one who had ever been able to make her come. Though to be fair, she hadn't really ever given anyone but Jimmy a chance to try.

She was tight, yes—but she was twenty-seven years old, for crying out loud! It'd never even crossed her mind that he'd be able to tell she hadn't been ridden countless times and put away damp. He was obviously stunned, and she certainly hadn't meant to give him such a shock. Damn, talk about startling the hell out of a guy.

He didn't laugh, didn't smile—didn't so much as move a muscle except for the ticking in his clenched jaw. "Oh, I can tell, sweetheart. Believe me. You actually thought I wouldn't know once I was buried up your cunt? Hell, you can't be that fucking naïve! I've had virgins who weren't this friggin' tight!"

She blinked at the accusation in his words, as if he were expecting some outraged father with a shotgun at his back any second now. Her gaze darted away, focusing on a point past his right shoulder. "Of course I didn't think you'd be able to tell. Think about it, Ryan. I'm twenty-seven, not sixteen! I didn't think this would be an issue," she told him in a low voice, wishing like hell he'd just get on with it already. Just the feel of that beautiful cock buried deep inside of her, stretching her so wonderfully wide, filling her to the absolute limit, was better than anything she'd ever experienced.

Her eyes found his again, and Ryan felt himself falling into their bewitching swirls of color. "Don't let this matter, Ryan. *Please*. Don't stop, not now."

"It does matter, damn it. Don't think you can act like it doesn't." He wanted to yell at her some more, anything to keep from thinking about the fact that he'd just all but busted through her cunt, but his mouth brushed hers, his chest aching with unsettling emotion while his body throbbed painfully. The feel of her gripping him so tightly, her drenched pussy gloving him perfectly, was driving him straight to that place that he feared.

It was dark and dangerous; something that went far beyond mere physical need. He didn't trust himself, and he didn't know what in the hell to do about it. All he wanted was to go wild on her and screw her brains out, right through the plaster at her back. "Damn it," he grunted, his voice thick with lust and despair. "I'm the last person in the world you should be wasting yourself on, Shea."

She leaned toward him and her lips touched his in the sweetest, softest kiss he'd ever had. Ryan felt the shocking sensation shoot straight down to the root of his dick, then thicken and surge its way up toward the broad tip. *Oh shit.* He was gonna come and he hadn't even fucked her yet. In a panic, he ripped his lips away from hers, barely holding himself together.

She touched his mouth with wonder, and her own curled in a fey smile that made him wonder how he'd ever survived this long without her. "I don't consider it a waste, Ry. You're exactly what I want, what I've been waiting for. Believe me—I'm right where I want to be. Yeah, I could have a lot more experience than I do—but it was my choice, just like *this* is my choice. I'm a grown woman and I know what I want—and what I want is *you*."

His forehead dropped to hers. Shit, he couldn't get his head around it. How had he gotten to this point, with his cock crammed up inside of Shea so deep she could probably feel it at the back of her throat? Where was his control? He should pull out and get his filthy hands off of her, but he knew it'd kill him if he did.

Then Shea ran her fingers through his hair again, shifting slightly, and her cream-soaked pussy sucked him deeper, pulling a strange, sob-like sound from his throat.

"Hey," she teased, the innocent trying to soothe the slut, "it's okay. Trust me, Ry, if you'd been dating the same geeks I have, you'd have been holding out some too."

How she managed to make him laugh at the most emotionally intense moment of his life, he'd never know. But he was suddenly filled with a warm, piercing relief and profound gratitude that he was *the one inside of her*, and not one of those measly, limp-dicked little bastards she'd dated before.

Trying not to hurt her, Ryan slowly withdrew from her body until only the head of his cock remained within the swollen, stretched rim of her vulva, and then he worked himself back up into her, forcing his way in. She was getting hotter, slicker, soaking him—all creamy and warm and wet—and the feeling of finally being inside of her was the most incredible thing he'd ever experienced. Shea was every fantasy and adolescent wet dream he'd ever had, innocent and seductively sensual, the erotic contradiction wearing his control to the breaking point.

Again he moved out and back in, his movements deliberately careful, but Shea wasn't having it. She loved the slow, precise feeling of his thick erection moving inside of her, all those long, vein-ridged inches of cock stretching her open, pulling her apart. But more than that, she wanted him wild and out of control again. She wanted him to find pleasure without worrying he was hurting her, without this careful restraint.

"Ryan," she moaned against his mouth, biting gently at his bottom lip. "Ry, you can let go. I'm not going to break if you take me hard. God, I want you to! I want it the way I've always read it could be. Show me how it can really be, Ry. *Show me.*"

And just like that, his caution broke. "*Oh fuck,*" he groaned helplessly, pinning her hard to the wall, trapping her as his body pulled out and then rammed back in with a hard scraping motion that raked her inner walls with pleasure.

She heard someone release a broken shout, vaguely wondering if the erotic cry had come from her. Then he did it again, only this time harder, faster, slamming her with his cock, and suddenly she was lost in the fury and depth of his strokes.

Ryan took her again and again, his big body hard and hungry, his cock ruthless, plunging and withdrawing until he thought he'd die from the pleasure of fucking her.

He wanted it to go on forever, but it was too good, too hot, too everything. His balls tightened as his stomach muscles clenched, signaling his release, and he wanted her there with him, milking him dry to the very end. "Come," he ordered hoarsely, his mouth hot and damp, almost biting against the side of her neck.

Ryan lifted her higher, angling his body so that each deep thrust worked him against her clit, pushing her where he wanted her, grinding against her with expert pressure and friction. "I wanna feel you creaming around my cock this time, Shea. Next time I'm gonna swallow it down my throat again, just like last night, but this time I want your cunt sucking me tight while I fill you up. *Come on, baby.*"

He pulled out, shoved back in, pulled out, crammed deeper, and suddenly she was flying, the pleasure exploding through her in a warm, violent rush, forced out of her by his words and his body.

He felt the hard tension of her tightening passage, and then all those exquisite little muscles were squeezing his naked cock in a delicious rhythm that ripped his orgasm right out of him.

Ryan came with a rough shout, banging her body against the wall as he spilled and spilled and spilled, until he thought she'd drained him of everything, until he could barely stand. His muscles shook, taxed from the force of his release, and he gave a masculine grunt of horror at the feel of his legs giving out. They slumped down the wall together. He caught himself hard on his knees, gripping her bottom tightly so as not to pull out of her sweet, cum-filled pussy, not yet ready to break the intimate contact.

Hell, he thought with a low groan. He'd never be ready. This was some serious, whacked out, scary shit. He felt like he'd just been turned inside out, completely exposed, and not just physically. His skin and shields had been peeled away, and now everything was out in the open in the rawest way he could've imagined.

It was worse than he'd feared, this insane connection they shared — but then it was so much more.

It was the most incredible sex he'd ever had, red hot and raging, completely uncontrollable. Seriously mind-blowing. Shit, he felt like he'd just had a friggin' epiphany. So what in the hell was he supposed to do now? He could always try running again. But damn it, he didn't want to. What he wanted was to sink even deeper inside of her and stay that way forever.

In his arms, Shea stirred against him, a low hum of satisfaction purring in the back of her throat. "Mmm," she sighed. "God, that was so awesome. I think I felt the earth move."

Ryan couldn't stop the silly grin that found its way through the fog of mind-numbing sensation. "Awesome?" he asked teasingly, nudging her face up with his own so he could look at her. Her skin was rosy and flushed, slightly damp. She was so beautiful, the sexiest damn thing he'd ever seen, and she was his. *Oh, God.* It hit him like a Mack truck in the center of his chest, knocking the wind right out of him. She was his. Her cunt, her mouth, her sweetness — *everything was all his!* "Damn, woman," he groaned shakily, trying to regain his balance. "You nearly killed me."

She smiled, looking extremely pleased with herself — and with him. "So then you weren't disappointed?"

Ryan's own smile disappeared, replaced by a deep, intense look of tenderness. "You could never disappoint me." With the softest of touches, he kissed her temple, the alluring curve of her cheek. "God, you're so soft, so sweet. I'm so damn fucking fascinated by you," he growled, knowing he meant every word and touch, no matter how badly they terrified him. "I always have been. So don't even think of trying to throw me out again, because I'm not going anywhere, lady."

Chapter Six

Ryan carefully disengaged their bodies while Shea squirmed in his arms, his blood pumping hard from the wild kisses she playfully planted over his face and throat. Torn between smiling at her eagerness and groaning from the fresh surge of lust pounding through his body, he removed the few articles of clothing they were still wearing as he stumbled his way into the bathroom, his hands gripping the sweet cheeks of her ass to keep her against him. With one hand he reached into the shower to get the water running hot, and when the air filled with steam, he carried Shea beneath the warm spray.

What the hell had he done? His stunningly uncharacteristic words stormed through his brain, but he couldn't find a way to take them back.

Hell, he didn't want to take them back—didn't want to take any of it back.

And why in God's name wasn't he more upset about it? It'd been years since he'd allowed himself to feel anything beyond the physical pleasure a good fuck could afford—and the last time had been a total disaster. Had, in fact, damn near altered the entire course of his life.

Why wasn't he pissed at his loss of control, rather than strangely warm inside at the thought that he'd finally had her—and planned on having her again and again? Granted, she'd been more than a good fuck. Despite her inexperience, Shea had been the best fuck he'd ever had. Christ, if she got any better, he'd be a dead man.

She sighed, and he couldn't help but smile at the soft, inaudible sound. Hell, he was so obsessed, she could breathe and he'd hear it.

He felt like one of the addicts he so often busted during the course of his investigations. Highly successful professionals who should've known better, but once they got that taste of their personal paradise, all they could think about was getting it again. They sought heaven by whatever means necessary—no matter how much of a hell it landed them in.

Only his heaven wasn't going to be found in any illegal substance. No, it was soft and sweet, snuggled up against his chest, all but wrapped around his body in a way that said she didn't ever want to let go. And if that didn't send him running, then nothing would. Strange as it was, the only thing he could think about was pulling her closer, pushing back into the addictive depths of her cunt, and never leaving.

And wasn't this why he'd struggled so hard to stay away from her? Hadn't he known, deep down, that fucking this woman was going to be about a hell of a lot more than sex, and take him someplace completely unexpected?

He'd known last night, when he'd gone to lie down on her sofa and found himself dialing Hannah's cell phone, needing answers to the riddle that she'd become. The intoxicating puzzle that he wanted to unravel, piece by piece, until he could figure out just what made her tick. On one level, it was the investigator in him—but most importantly it was the man. The man wanted to get under her guard, just like she'd crawled under his, and push her farther than anyone ever had before. He wanted to get to the core of Shea Dresden...uncover all her little secrets…and claim her in the most primal, primitive way a man could stake his claim.

And the call with Hannah hadn't been easy. Not that he'd expected her to break confidence with Shea and spill it all, no matter how close he and Hannah were, but he hadn't counted on the pangs of conscience she'd invoked. He'd damned near blushed when she'd started reading him the riot act.

"So what are you looking for here, Ry? Because I don't think you're going to like what I've got to say."

"Shit, why do women always have to make everything so damn difficult?" he'd muttered, stretching out across Shea's thankfully long sofa, smelling her subtle scent on the scarlet cushion behind his head and the soft chenille throw he'd tossed over his even longer body. "All I want is to know—to try to understand—ah shit, I don't know what I called you for. Just forget it."

"She's really gotten to you, hasn't she?"

"And wouldn't you love it if she had?"

"Don't sneer at me, Ry. If I didn't think you two were perfect for each other, I could've warned her off you long ago. Trust me, you big jerk, it's been hell trying to paint you as anything other than an oversexed playboy."

He snorted. "What the hell? You been keeping tabs on my love life, Hannah?"

"Okay, genius, let's see if you can figure this one out on your own? Now that you've seen her bedroom, and you know where her bed is, why don't you put two-and-two together in that crime-solving brain of yours and explain to me why she might have that impression of you?"

He'd grunted, cursing women for the twisted riddles they spoke in, when it suddenly dawned on him. Ah shit. *Shit. Shit. Shit.* Her fucking bed was against the same wall as his. The same wall his bed slammed into every damn time he brought home a woman to screw. The same thin wall that probably bled every damn sound right through its cheap-ass drywall. *Son-of-a-bitch.*

He'd made a low, groaning curse, and Hannah had clucked softly on the other end. "Yeah, you got it, big guy. You've been giving her quite the show lately."

"Shit, I never even thought of that." He'd cringed, thinking of his desperate attempts lately to screw her out of his system. Hell, he'd probably slept with five different women just in the last month, trying to work his way out of this obsession for Shea.

Hannah's sigh had been deep and heavy, fully exaggerated. "I swear, Ry, sometimes you can be so damn dense when it comes to women."

He'd shut his eyes and tried to remember what Shea might have heard, but his mind was a blank. The women had been poor attempts to convince himself that what Shea made him feel wasn't any different from any other woman, but it hadn't worked. No amount of raunchy, mindless screwing had done the job.

Hell, he'd been fantasizing about Shea the entire damn time he'd been pounding into them anyway. But fuck, he hated the thought of her hearing him with another woman. It felt like a betrayal, though he knew he didn't owe her a damn thing at this point. It's not like he'd made her any promises. He'd spent the last three months doing his best to ignore her, so how could what he'd done have been so bad?

But it felt bad, damn it, and he knew in his gut that it had felt bad to Shea. He couldn't even imagine what his reaction would've been if he'd heard her nailing some guy, her bed banging against the wall, her raw, muffled cries of climax slamming into his brain. Shit, he'd have probably knocked her damn door down and beaten the jerk senseless.

And wasn't that possessive fire burning in his gut one of the reasons he'd tried so damn hard to stay away from her?

"Look, I didn't want to say anything because this really isn't my business, but if I keep leaving you to your own devices, you're going to dig yourself so far into a hole you won't ever be able to get back out."

"Christ, you gonna give me pointers on sex now, Hannah? I thought we'd already covered the fact that I had that covered back when you caught me playing doctor with Susie Jenkins?"

"Oh, you know how to make them happy in bed. I'm not doubting you there, stud boy. I've seen the way they drag their tongues around after you. But when it comes to anything beyond sex, you're pathetic. Geez, you don't even notice a woman unless you're planning on nailing her, and once you've had her, you never give her the time of day again."

"Damn it, I never make promises that I—"

"Shut up, Ry. I'm not saying it's not their own faults, because I know you always make it perfectly clear you're not interested in getting emotionally involved with any of them. You're just out to have some fun, blow off some steam, but that doesn't mean they don't go in thinking they'll be the ones to change your mind. You know, rock your world and all that."

"Is there a point to all this?"

"Yeah," she'd drawled, "because the sad fact remains that you simply don't know crappola about dealing with women outside of anything sexual."

And I've got a damn good reason, he'd thought, but only said, "I deal with you just fine."

She'd sighed over the line. "I don't count, Ry. We're practically family. The thought of us boinking probably sounds as gross to you as it does to me."

"Jesus, woman" he'd groaned, "don't even talk about that shit. It'd be like doing my sister."

Hannah had laughed, knowing she'd scored a hit with that one. "See, you get my point. You've never even thought about me as a woman, so you haven't shut yourself off from me...*like you've done with every other female you've known since college*."

She didn't say since Kelly, so he supposed he should at least be thankful for that, but he was still pissed that she'd scored a direct hit with that one too.

"Just what in the hell is the point of all this? I thought you were trying to play matchmaker, not give me a lecture on my obvious lack of charm."

"What I'm trying to tell you is that you cannot be a macho idiot with this woman and let her get away. Trust me, if you do, it'll be the biggest mistake of your entire life."

The biggest mistake of his life...

Shea swayed forward, the fiercely erotic touch of her wet nipples against his chest pulling him painfully back to the present. His arms instinctively tightened, needing to feel her closeness as the water continued to stream down on them, Hannah's unsettling words replaying repeatedly, echoing eerily in his head. No…he hadn't let her get away. At least, not this time.

But just look at what he'd done, damn it.

He should have been taking care of her, keeping his bastard hands to himself, but no. No, he'd just slammed her against her bedroom wall, fucked the hell out of her, and filled her full of cum. No romance. No sweet words. He'd just lifted her up and rammed his cock into her as hard as he could—mindless to everything but gaining the satisfaction he'd known he would find inside of her. The teeth-grinding, heart-pumping, complete overload of sensation that only she could give him.

He felt sick. Not at what had happened, but because he was so damn happy about it. He knew, after the hell she'd just been through with Spalding, that he'd had no right touching her—and sure as hell not today. But instead of leaving her alone, like he should have, he'd ended up taking her right there with the finesse of a juggernaut. Damn, he wanted to kick his own ass.

And he wanted to keep holding her close, keep screwing her senseless, keep staking his claim again and again.

For the rest of the damn day.

Every day.

Forever.

Oh, man, he had this so bad. Who the fuck had he been trying to fool? He wasn't going to run, and he wasn't going to let her go. He was going to act just like the ruthless bastard he knew he was and dig his claws into her for good.

Everything about Shea twisted him with need, and he was not a man to twist and moan for any woman, no matter how good she looked. Until now. And it wasn't just her looks, damn it, but the whole package that he wanted—the whole woman. He wanted to pound himself inside of *her* again and again—not just her body, but *her*—until he'd affected her in the same ways she was changing him.

Like any sane man, he wanted those changes about as much as he wanted his damn dick cut off. He'd always liked his life just fine the way it was. Hell, he'd learned early on that he didn't need some woman screwing with it, no matter how badly he wanted to screw around with her. He liked being in control. Liked doing what he wanted, when he wanted. Liked the variety of women who'd always been readily available to him. Liked the fact that he could fuck them and forget them without ever suffering a single second of emotional involvement.

And now he was neck deep in it.

Shea's hands clutched at his broad shoulders while she struggled against the primal urge to sink her teeth into his warm flesh. She wanted to just swallow him down—just fill herself up on him. She clung to him, mentally lecturing herself for holding him in such a death grip, afraid she was going to end up scaring him away.

But Ryan wasn't running. He just held her close, as if he never meant to let her go—his hard cock trapped between their stomachs—the silver hoop in her navel digging deliciously into his swollen flesh.

Her sweet lips and soft hands shredded his control, until he finally couldn't take it anymore. "Shea, please stop, baby. I'm trying not to get too rough with you, but you're—"

"That...sounds...fine—" she stuttered on an uneven breath, then tried again. "God, that's sounds more than fine. It sounds fabulous. So will you stop worrying that I'm going to shatter any second now? You're starting to give me a complex."

He smiled at her disgruntled tone and stroked his cheek against the silky top of her head, holding her so the warm water fell directly over her sore body. Damn, would he ever understand this woman? He was trying to offer the gentle lovemaking she deserved, and she was all but demanding he fuck her senseless again.

"A complex?" he laughed, running his hands over the slick flesh of her body, loving the feel of her beneath his palms. She fit against him as if she'd been made just for this—just for him. "Well, we can't have that, can we?"

"No," she moaned, trying to get closer, wanting to just crawl up inside of him. "I never knew it would be so amazing, even after wanting you for so long. Then you said those really incredible things to me and now I can't help it. I need more," she added with a small groan, feeling like she'd go crazy if she didn't get him back inside of her—filling her up—that very instant.

She had the sexiest man ever made naked in her shower, and all she could think about were the wonderfully wicked things she wanted to be doing to his gorgeous body. She needed to be touching him with her hands and mouth—going down on her knees for a taste of that giant, beautiful cock—while she had the chance!

Ryan laughed a low, deep rumble that shook her against his chest, the relief spearing through him as sharp as it was satisfying. "You are an insatiable little thing, aren't you?" he murmured around a smile, settling her on her feet, keeping her body pressed against his own with one arm behind her back. With his other hand, he lifted her chin, forcing her to look up at him. "And to think for a minute there I was almost worried I might've broken you or something," he teased, blue eyes sparkling, long lashes spiked with water.

She blushed, looking delightfully pink under the warm spray of the shower, but her eyes were dark and hungry. "I'm tougher than I look," she quipped in a husky murmur, and just like that, Ryan felt himself losing it.

He kissed the tip of her nose, her eyelids, then brushed the softest of kisses across her pink mouth while trying to rein himself in. "God, Shea," he groaned a little shakily. "Don't tempt me, honey, or I'm likely to push you up against this shower wall and take you again right now, no matter how sore you are."

"Yeah? I like the sound of that. I've never had slippery, wet sex in the shower before. And who ever said I was too sore? I could never be too sore for you, Ry."

Hell, she was gonna be the death of him.

Ryan smiled down at her, ridiculously happy just to be with her, finding her every bit as fascinating as he'd claimed. His eyes gleamed with devilish intent while his big hands kneaded her naked backside, loving the way her firm flesh filled his palms. "You've hardly ever had sex *anywhere* before, you little tease, but you need some downtime before I fuck you again."

The only thing Shea knew she needed was Ryan. Forget about being sore. Who could give a crud about a little discomfort when Ryan McCall was primed and ready? The beauty of his hard-muscled body rivaled the perfection of any Ancient Greek statue she'd ever seen— only he wasn't made of stone. Well, at least not all of him. With a soft sigh of longing, she pressed against him, rubbing her torso against his wonderfully obvious, enormous erection.

"You're the only thing I need." She kissed his jaw, reached up on tiptoe and nipped the side of his neck, loving the warm, salty taste of his skin. "Again. Right here, so I'll know this isn't a dream."

"That's it," he grunted with a strained expression, holding her away from him so he could think straight, or at least try to. God knew it wasn't easy around this woman. "You're pushing me, Shea, and I'm trying to do the right thing here."

She smiled wickedly, feeling free and alive with electricity, as if her entire body were humming with light and energy. "Yeah? And what if I told you I wanted you to do me instead?"

Ryan's eyes narrowed at her boldness. "I'd say you're asking for more than you can take right now, little one." His voice went lower as his eyes traveled slowly down her body, his big hands running up and down her sides, molding over her narrow hips. Droplets of water slid down her stomach, over her sexy pierced navel, clinging to the soft, dark curls between her legs. He couldn't resist tweaking those curls with his fingers, wanting to bury his face right there and eat her alive. "Trust me, Shea. You have no idea what I've been fantasizing about doing to you for the past three hell-filled months. And that was before I knew what a hot little fuck you are."

She quivered before him, giving herself away as her long lashes lowered over the most dangerous pair of bedroom eyes he'd ever seen. It was all he could do to choke back a wolfish smile of cocky satisfaction.

Who would've ever thought that shy, intellectual Shea would get turned on by a guy talking dirty to her? Of course, the blatant fact that he intended to be the only man giving her the dirty talk wasn't lost on him. In fact, he was looking forward to every single second of it.

The sensuous press of her naked breasts against his chest brought his attention back to the problem at hand as she moved against him.

"I want you for as long as I can have you." She swallowed and licked her lips, her white teeth biting into the pouty flesh of the bottom one. "If that means being sore, I don't care. It isn't going to stop me from having you," she laughed with a sultry smile. "You'd be surprised what types of things I've thought about doing *to you*. Who knows—maybe you'll be the one who's shocked?"

Jesus, who was this woman? His muscles tightened with the effort of holding back, while the knot in his dick tripled in need. "Damn it, I *do* care." His tone took on an angry edge as he stroked the slight bruise on her cheekbone. "You've already had a hell of a weekend, babe, and that was before I got my hands on you."

She shot him a hot look of frustration, then lowered her chin, mumbling something under her breath. Ryan heard the soft grumble of her voice, but couldn't understand the muttered words over the hot spray of the water. "Why do women always do that?" he drawled—his chest rumbling with soft laughter.

Shea blinked up at him. "Do what?"

The corners of his sexy mouth lifted. "Talk to themselves."

"Because men never listen?" she offered sweetly, fine black brows rising over sparkling gray eyes.

His big, rough hands trailed possessively up and down the line of her spine, resting against the soft, alluring swell at the top of her ass. "I listen to you."

"Uh-huh. Which is why you stayed when I told you to leave."

He leaned down and nipped the full flesh of her bottom lip with his strong teeth, knowing the sharp stab of sensation would shoot straight down to the empty core of her cunt. She trembled in his arms, and he had to bite back another wolfish grin. "Yeah, but you wanted me to stay."

Her fingers curved around his hips, trying to pull him into her, wanting to feel the press of that magnificent, engorged cock against her fluttering belly. "And right now I want you to fuck me."

The husky words drilled straight through his brain, and he had to lock his damn knees against the need to do just that. Brushing his mouth across hers, he whispered, "I already told you, sweetheart. Not yet."

Shea groaned with defeat and pulled out of his arms, quickly making use of the soap, shampoo, and conditioner, knowing he was glued to her every movement and liking the sexy feeling of power that knowledge gave her. Feminists could go on all day and night about the negative aspects of stereotyping women as sex objects, but as an educated female, and a quite brilliant one at that, Shea appreciated the fact that there were times when it felt good to know a man was looking at your body and thinking about nothing other than how badly he wanted it.

Of course, it had to be the right man, and Ryan McCall was definitely that, even if he was starting to tick her off. Just because she was a little inexperienced didn't mean she was fragile, and she sure as hell didn't want to be handled with kid gloves, especially by him!

They finished in a heavy silence, the air between them even heavier with sexual undercurrents. Shea turned to step out of the shower, giving him a perfect view of her sweet little heart-shaped ass, and he groaned under his breath.

Damn. He'd never seen anything like it, and his cock paid homage to such a beautiful sight by kicking up another notch. *Whoa boy, down.* He ached from his head to his toes, and it was an agonizing torment not to give in and give her exactly what she was asking for.

She handed him a fluffy white towel as he stepped out behind her, her eyes narrowed in irritation. "Who would've thought a guy with your wicked reputation would be such a spoilsport?"

His eyes fastened hot and hungry on her rosy breasts, following the movements of her towel as she dried them. "I want you back in bed," he said suddenly, and there was no disguising the thick, urgent sound of need in his voice.

Those stormy eyes of hers went heavy in response, firing his blood even more. Her breath rushed through her slightly parted, soft pink lips. "Yeah? Have you changed your mind then?"

Her tongue flicked her bottom lip again, snaring his gaze, making him think of things of his own he had for her to flick and lick. "The bed, Shea," he ordered roughly, herding her in that direction with his big body. "First you rest, then I'll show you what a sport I can be."

The look she sent over her shoulder was as hungry as his. "Promise?"

This time, his eyes gleamed. "Sweetheart, by the time I'm done with you, neither one of us may walk for a week."

Chapter Seven

When they lay back down among the soft white linens of Shea's bed, Ryan forced himself to be gentle, soothing, lover-like, but it was hard as hell with her rubbing her naked body all over his. Finally he got them settled beneath the sheet, both their heads sharing the same pillow while they stared into each other's eyes, trying to make sense out of everything that was happening to them.

With one blunt fingertip, Ryan traced the delicate features of her face. A fey face that was so precious to him—that had been since he'd first seen it. Her brows were finely arched over the biggest gray-blue eyes he'd ever seen, her lashes long and thick, cheekbones high, nose small and pert, skin a creamy pale gold with a light sprinkling of freckles across the bridge of her nose.

And her mouth.

Damn, just looking at those soft, lush lips made him ache with erotic thoughts of twisting his hands into the soft mass of her silky, dark curls and dragging her down to where he wanted her the most. He could just imagine how sweet it would feel sinking past those lips, shocking a look of stunned surprise from those big eyes as he pushed his cock deep. With painstaking detail, he'd tell her how to stroke him with her soft, pink tongue, tease the head of his cock with those petal-like lips, and then suck him into that sweet little mouth until he came hot and wet and scalding down her throat.

Then again, Ryan thought with a wry grin, Shea was the most naturally sexual woman he'd ever known, despite her relative inexperience. He probably wouldn't have to teach her a damn thing.

Just thinking about it had him hard and throbbing all over again. She shot his control to hell, until he didn't think he'd ever be able to be near her and not ache to bury himself up inside her sticky sweet cunt. The woman just affected him, no two ways about it, and now that he'd had her — well, now her effect was even stronger.

Ryan still couldn't believe he'd finally drilled his cock into that beautiful pussy. He wanted to brand her as his so that every guy out there, even her snot-nosed poets and artists, would know she was his.

He wasn't going to let her forget it.

If he had to, he'd keep her physically exhausted and pulsing with pleasure for the rest of his life, but Shea Dresden was not getting rid of him. Ryan hoped like hell she realized what she'd gotten herself into. It wasn't just that she'd been so hungry for a good, hard, mind-shattering fuck, and that he'd been the first man to really give her one. She was *his* in a way that went beyond the physical. He'd tried to run from it, but this strange connection had been creeping up on him from the moment they'd first met.

Running from it hadn't helped. Avoiding her hadn't helped. Now that he'd had her, there was no way in hell he could go back. Damn, he didn't even want to.

But what did Shea want?

Suddenly Ryan was very much aware of the fact that she'd yet to say anything about the future. Oh, she'd said she wanted him, and almost even said she loved him, he thought, but then that had been in the passion of the moment last night—and he knew not to bet too much on things spoken at a time like that.

What did she really want from him? She was staring back at him across the soft white cotton pillowcase, looking at him with all the love in the world shining in her eyes, or was he just seeing what he wanted to see? Was he just an adventure for her? A walk on the wild side before she settled down with some nice academic type and raised little poet laureates? *Like hell.* No matter what she'd planned before, Ryan was going to make it infinitely clear that her future was with him now.

Hell if he knew how it'd happened, but there was no stopping it.

Shea snuggled deeper into the pillow, her legs shifting against his, moving her body closer to his, which was exactly where he wanted it. The sheet dipped, revealing one puffy pink nipple, and he couldn't resist stroking it with his thumb, watching the way it tightened into a hard little bud with the first touch of his skin. He wanted to take it between his teeth and tease her until she was ready to come just from having him suck on her beautiful tits.

Then he flicked his gaze up and caught a strange look of embarrassment in her eyes. Jesus, after everything else they'd done, he couldn't believe she'd get shy about her breasts, and the look went straight to his heart.

"What are you thinking about?" he asked, his deep voice still rough with physical satisfaction.

"Just that they're not, um, really your type." She swallowed thickly and tried for a smile, but he could tell it was forced. "I mean—well, I'm not blind, Ry. I've seen the kinds of figures you like. They're always tall and built and curvy. I must look like a scrawny tomboy compared to what you're used to."

He groaned silently in his head, wondering just how many women she'd actually seen him with. Christ, no wonder she was making remarks about not being his type. If she'd gotten a good look at any of his dates, she probably thought he was attracted to nothing more than long legs and big tits. Hell, that's what *he'd* thought he was attracted to, at least until he'd gotten a look at her.

Now the only type he liked was Shea, end of story.

There wasn't anything else for him.

But that wasn't how she saw it, and it certainly wasn't how she'd heard it if Hannah was right and she'd listened to him nailing those other women. He couldn't stop reminding himself that she'd heard him in action, thinking of how awful that must have been for her if she really did care about him. God, just the thought of it made him sick.

Not really knowing what to say, he laughed hoarsely and drawled, "A tomboy?"

"Yeah. All brains and no bod. That's me."

Ryan couldn't understand how she could actually believe such a thing, and it infuriated him to hear her put herself down that way. Didn't the idiot woman know how fucking blown over he was by her? How friggin' obsessed? On the verge of lovesick, for God's sake!

"You know, maybe you are blind, Shea. In case it escaped your notice, just looking at you makes me harder than a fucking spike—harder than I've ever been before. You're small and sexy and beautiful, and you have the prettiest little pink cu—oomph," a pillow hit him smack in the face, "that I've ever seen," he finished with a soft laugh.

Though she flushed at his words, she looked away, clearly not believing him. Ryan caught her chin with his fingers and brought her eyes back to his. "I may be a lot of things, Shea, but I'm not a liar. I've never wanted anything the way I've wanted you. I tried like hell to ignore you, but you were always there, filling my mind every minute of every day and night."

She swallowed hard, mesmerized by the way his eyes traveled over her so hotly, his gaze fierce and possessive as he pulled the sheet away, slowly revealing her. She knew she blushed from her roots to her toes, but she was too overwhelmed by his words to worry about being embarrassed.

"And now that I've had you," he added in a low, gruff tone, "I only want you more." He lowered his head, stroking the flat of his tongue across her nipple while holding her warm gaze. Her breath sucked in and her pupils nearly swallowed the gray of her eyes, and so he did it again, curling his tongue around the tip for a hard, wet suck. When he got the reaction he wanted and she cried out, he said, "I want to suck on these beautiful tits, stuffing my mouth full of them, every chance I get, Shea. Almost as much as I want to fuck you, over and over and over, until you've grown so used to the feel of my cock crammed up inside of you that your cunt aches without it. I want you to feel empty and hollow and hungry, waiting for the next time I'm going to fill you up."

Her eyes stormed, flashes of gray and black and blue, raging like a tempest at sea. With her breath hitching, she licked her lips in a nervous gesture that made him moan. "Then why did you run from me?"

His gold-stubbled cheeks went hot with color. "I didn't run," he muttered, and they both knew he was lying through his teeth.

Shea rolled her eyes at him. "Hah, McCall!"

"Men don't run, babe. We fight and fondle and fuck, but we sure as hell don't run."

"Hmm. Sure looked like running to me."

He shook his head with chagrin, touching the corner of her mouth with his thumb. "Yeah, well, maybe you just scared the hell outta me."

She went still beside him. "Yeah? And why is that?"

Damn it, what the hell was he doing, saying crap like that, baring his soul? It was too much, all of this, just like he'd known it would be. He couldn't even think straight. Everything was breaking him open. All the intimate little details that he'd dreamed about for weeks. The feel of her, the smell, the taste. Everything about the woman was too damn addictive.

But he couldn't fight it. What was the friggin' point? No, he was digging in. Staking a claim. Now. Here. This very moment. Hell, it'd been staked the moment he shoved his cock into her.

Shea watched him with eyes that looked far wiser than her years, her keen intelligence adding yet another dimension to his fascination. He didn't know what she saw in his fierce expression, but it was evidently enough for her to know not to press him for answers and explanations. Instead, she pressed her warm, liquid cunt against his thigh and draped her slender leg over his hip.

"I'm already aching and empty," she whispered with naked honesty, loving the warm, muscled feel of him beneath her hands as she stroked his wide shoulders, his arms, his chest. She wanted to touch all of him at once. "You know I always am—that I'm always hungry for you. Starved. So take me again, Ry. Come on, I dare you."

He smiled a lopsided grin that made him look devastatingly boyish, erasing the lines of tension from his handsome face. Then his warm, calloused palm slid over her mound, cupping her, pushing her to her back as he rose to his elbow beside her. "As much as I want to be buried deep in this perfect pussy of yours, we really shouldn't right now," he explained in a smoky rasp, leaning down to kiss her parted lips, teasing her with slow strokes of his tongue. "I was too rough with you, Shea. You're still so swollen. I know you must be sore, babe." His voice hardened with conviction. "Damn it, I won't hurt you again."

"I don't care. I mean it," she argued, moving against his hand. "And you're really starting to piss me off about this. I'm not some fragile little china doll that's gonna break if you play too rough, Ry. I want you. Right now. I want this!"

Unable to help himself, and not really wanting to, he allowed his fingers to press deeper, stroking her tender lips, delving between the soft, velvety folds of skin. He ached for the feel of her on his tongue again, the intimate taste of her in his mouth. Her scent was filling his head, making his mouth water and his stomach cramp with need.

Suddenly he was rising up beside her, tossing the sheet over the end of the bed. "Open your legs for me," he grunted huskily. His eyes fastened on her soft curls, watching the way they snared his fingers, the way they glistened with her slick moisture.

"Now?" Her voice was unsteady, her body restless as she shifted atop the cool sheet. She knew it was a stupid question, but her normally oh-so-clever mind wasn't working too well at the moment. Maybe she was blowing brain cells like an addict, overdosing on orgasms, but who cared? She'd always had more brains than she knew what to do with; she could afford to lose a little in the name of mindless sexual gratification.

Rising to his knees, Ryan said it again, this time as an order, something not to be denied. "Spread your legs for me, Shea. I want to look at you." After all her brazen demands, it was so cute to see her look suddenly embarrassed. "I want to get a nice close shot of this sexy little cunt you keep begging me to fuck."

"Yeah?" she asked, knowing she sounded like a naïve idiot, but unable to get over how exposed she'd feel in the bright light of day. Last night was one thing, in the soft, mellow shadows, but Ryan looked like he wanted to shine a spotlight between her legs and start taking notes. "Maybe we should, um, turn off the lights first."

Ryan's eyes blazed, all sparks and blue flaming fire. "Hell no. I want to be able to look at you, Shea. I've dreamed about laying you down like this and spreading you open since I first saw you in that friggin' wet dream you call a bikini. Come on. Open up for me nice and wide. I'll make you feel better. I promise."

Slowly, she did as he asked, unable to deny the dark thrill of wonder at what he would do to her this time as he moved purposefully between her legs. Oh, she'd read about oral sex tons of times, in searing, delicious detail— but she'd never imagined it would feel as incredible as it did, or that he'd seem to enjoy eating her just as much as she enjoyed being eaten. Her thighs trembled, but she forced them wider. Then his hands were catching her behind her knees, forcing them out at her sides, and Shea found herself spread-eagled, completely exposed.

A small, helpless sound of embarrassment broke from her throat, but Ryan only held her tighter as she instinctively tried to bring her knees together. "God, look at you," he whispered hoarsely, feeling something in his chest clench hard with need.

With one hand, he separated her swollen lips, exposing the glistening vulva and clit hidden within—all that sweet, wet, pink flesh—and he made a rumbling, cat-like sound in the back of his throat. Ryan looked his fill of her cunt, while the fingers of his other hand stroked over her slow and knowingly. "So soft and pink and wet. You're drenched, sugar. All sticky and dripping like honey. And you smell like sin," he rasped, leaning close to take a deep, satisfying breath.

Shea lurched, shaking almost uncontrollably, her body trembling with need and anticipation. "Mmm...this is so much better than I thought it'd be," she stammered stupidly, knowing she was doing that whole twit thing again.

His body went tenser still. "Yeah? How many guys have you let touch you like this?" he whispered, pinching the lips of her cunt together, then spreading them far apart, opening her like a luscious piece of ripe fruit he couldn't wait to suck down his throat.

Her answering moan was ragged and long, the sultry sound of her pleasure pumping him with need. Ryan wanted her screaming again while she came, loving the way she was so powerless to control her reactions to him. It was only fitting, wasn't it? God only knew she had him as helpless as a fish on a hook, reeling him in faster and faster.

The morning air felt cool on Shea's exposed flesh, while the rest of her seemed to be steaming with heat. Ryan kept her spread wide, his blue gaze completely focused on the erotic sight before him—so intense she could all but feel the press of his eyes like a wicked touch. "Come on, honey. Tell me how many guys you've let get this close to this gorgeous little cunt before me. Five, ten, twenty?"

It was difficult to concentrate enough to think this thing through. Shea couldn't believe he'd ask her such a question. She could believe even less that he expected an answer. Unfortunately, the look on his face when he glanced at her told her he expected just that. "Uh-huh. No way. You would only laugh at me, Ry."

His fingers stroked her folds, rasping sensitive tissues with their calloused pads, teasing her clit and circling her still swollen opening in a dizzying rhythm that was making her delirious. "Not a chance, Shea."

"Um—well, no one really," she grudgingly admitted with no small amount of reluctance, her voice going breathless as she tried to explain. "Other than, you know, the guy I lost my virginity to. But we, um, didn't really do anything like this. I mean—he didn't go down on me or anything."

And she didn't really want to be telling him any of this, but it was just too difficult to think straight with her head tossing restlessly on the pillow while he fingered her with shallow thrusts of his middle finger. "I've dated guys," she moaned, feeling the absurd need to justify her inexperience, "and I'm not a prude—but I've just never really felt comfortable enough with anyone, or wanted them enough to let them—"

"So then you've never let any guy but me do this?" he growled, and his mouth closed over her with a luscious heat that speared straight from her cunt, to her middle, and up into the back of her throat, choking off her air.

Her body arched hard, a sharp, shocked scream of pleasure ripping from her chest. Ryan held her hips pinned to the bed with the strength of his hands until she settled. She was still new to this, so he tried to give her time to get used to the feel of his mouth on her. He didn't last long, though, and all too soon he couldn't keep his tongue from stroking boldly between her lips, collecting more of her erotic flavor. Warm melted sugar with a touch of spice. Hot and sweet and delicious.

"Damn, you taste incredible," he growled hungrily, his lips moving against her sopping, tender flesh, his tongue taking hungry licks between his words. "I always knew you'd be like this for me, your cunt so warm and wet. I want it all, sweetheart. Every single fucking drop. Come on and feed me."

"My...ah...um," she moaned, unable to keep her hips from moving against his face.

Ryan licked her with knowing expertise, learning her by touch and taste, and then his tongue slipped up inside of her with the evocative pressure of a kiss, plunging deep into the tiny slit as if he were taking her mouth.

"Oh shit!" she cried, the sound a keening expression of sexual awakening.

Shea writhed and thrashed beneath his skillful assault, and then the world was spinning as Ryan rolled their bodies, reversing their positions. The next thing she knew, she was straddling his face, his hands digging into her hips, forcing her down toward his waiting mouth. Her pussy was gushing, creaming down her thighs, aching to be crammed full of him.

"More," he demanded in a rough, sexy rasp. "Give me more. I want you to shove this beautiful little cunt in my face. I want my tongue up that sweet hole, fucking it, and I want it right now!"

It was too much. She felt too open in this position. Too exposed. "No, Ryan. Wait…"

His head lifted, just enough so he could run his tongue between her puffy lips, swirl it around the stiff bud of her clit. She stared down at him in shock and hunger. He stared up at her with all the force of his will, too sexy to resist, his lips wet with her juices.

"I want this, Shea. Stop screwing around with me. I want you sitting on my face, grinding that gorgeous cunt into my mouth, letting me tongue-fuck it. Now!"

She closed her eyes on a rough groan and lowered herself until she hovered just above his hungry mouth. He licked her again, gently suckled her labia between his lips, teasing her with the careful scrape of his teeth until she gasped, and a ragged whimper tore from her throat.

She couldn't fight it. Pleasure exploded inside of her as she followed his erotic command. She went weightless and had to reach out for the intricate wrought iron scrollwork of her headboard, needing something to hold on to, anything to anchor her to this world as Ryan's strong tongue plunged deeper, his mouth making seductive slurping sounds within the soaked wetness of her pussy. She was creaming like crazy and there was no help for it, not that he seemed to mind. His tongue went greedily after her streaming juices, plunging into her over and over, driving her with expert knowledge until she was moving against him, screaming and crying, her body pulsing as if the energy beneath her skin were going to burst pass the boundary of her body.

Just when she thought she couldn't take it a moment more, could no longer hold herself together, his tongue plunged again at the exact moment he pressed hard on her ripe, rosy clit with his calloused thumb. And then she was flying, her body breaking apart as she came in a violent rush. Raw, hoarse cries spilled from her throat, blending with Ryan's own savage sounds as his mouth ate at her pulsing flesh, greedily sucking the delicious juices from her cunt right down his throat.

He kept the exquisite pressure steady, kept her going until she went boneless above him, replete with drowsy satisfaction, her entire body still quaking with the aftershocks of ecstasy.

He'd meant only to give—wanted only to make her feel good—to drive her crazy with pleasure and show her just how much he wanted her. But her passionate response had pushed him too far, tumbling him past the ability to hold it together. He was mindless with need as he gave her warm, drenched pussy one last, lingering lick, then gripped her slim hips and forced her down his rigid body until she straddled his cock. Before he could remember to go slow, to be gentle with her, he bent his knees, planted his feet, and drove up into her.

The thrusting jolt of his penetration ripped another raw moan out of her, the low sound not entirely pleasure. But she was moving with him, lifting up with her knees, then working herself slowly back down, her hands braced against his hard abs.

Shea stared down at him, loving the feel of his golden, muscular body beneath her—*loving him*. It worried her that he might see it in her eyes and close himself off, but he wasn't even watching her face. More smoldering heat burned through her when she saw his eyes locked onto where his long, thick cock was pumping ruthlessly between her legs.

"You're so fucking small," he grunted, his fingers clenching around the silken skin of her hips. The air had gone heavy with their breathing and the wet sounds of his cock pounding into her, his tempo steadily increasing, as if he couldn't help himself. "Damn it, I'm...hell, I don't want to hurt you."

"You won't," she panted, and with a sly, sexy smile, she rose up and pushed down against him, forcing more of that incredible thickness into her body. She hadn't even taken half of him yet and already she felt stretched full. Her pussy throbbed with sharp pleasure and searing friction as he worked the top half in and out, her juices streaming down the unburied root of his cock, trickling over his tight sacs.

Ryan arched beneath her, sweat breaking out on his golden brow, his body shuddering from holding back the need to drive into her with a vicious lunge and plow deep, all the way to the hilt. "Try to take more of it. Please. Oh, God, I've got to feel all of you. Now, Shea. Take it now!"

She bit her lip, then surged down, pushing harder, and he rammed straight up into her tight, wet heat, holding her impaled, so far inside of her that she thought she felt him lodge against the blackness of her mind. She screamed and he only drove deeper, forcing her tight cunt to take every ruthless inch of him. Rough, animal-like sounds surged from his throat, rumbling through his chest as his hands grasped her hips, lifting her—up, up, up—and they both looked down to see him poised at her entrance.

His cock was incredibly long and flushed, thicker than the width of her wrist, throbbing with veins, the deep purplish-red skin now gleaming wetly with her juices. To Ryan, it looked barbaric, and he wondered how it didn't scare the hell out of her. But the soft catch of her breath revealed only need—a want as greedy, as insatiable as his own.

It was the most erotic thing he'd ever seen, the way her pretty little pink vulva stretched around him, ready, waiting to swallow him whole all over again.

"Ahhh—fuck," he groaned roughly, slamming her down on him again while he surged up, his hips leaving the bed. She sobbed, but then the noise that burst from his throat was sob-like too. Their bodies shuddered together, glistening with sweat, muscles taxed with desire.

Suddenly the room shifted as Ryan rolled them again, hips grinding against hips until he had her flat on her back. He pushed her legs up high and wide, his body surging deeper, jerking against her womb, forcing its way into her as deep as he could possibly go. Her spine and neck arched beneath him, those beautiful breasts swaying to his pounding rhythm, and he felt this savage need for her pierce sharply into his heart, digging beneath the hardened, once impenetrable layers of ice.

He drew out, then watched as he surged back into that narrow slit of flesh, feeling raw and possessive and hot enough to burn alive. "Keep your eyes on us," he growled. "I want you to watch me fucking you."

Shea's eyes shot open, locking on to where they joined. She lifted up on her elbows to better see, their foreheads nearly touching as together they watched his body surge in and out of hers.

"Damn, you feel so good. So tight and hot and wet. I love it, Shea. Christ, nothing's ever felt like this before. Never."

Ryan thrust harder, ramming into her, cramming in everything he had, and she cried out sharply. "Shit, is this too much for you?" he demanded in a gravelly voice, though the rhythm of his body hadn't changed. Hell, it hadn't even slowed down. He was as taken as she, her tight little cunt drawing him in, ripping away his legendary control.

Shea blew it all to hell. Reduced him to a savage, primitive male animal that could only take his woman again and again, claiming her in the most elemental way he knew. He was helpless, unable to temper his strength, his strong body using all its force to stake his claim. "Damn it, Shea, answer me! Is it too much?"

And if she said yes, what was he going to do about it?

"No," she panted. Her face was rosy and flushed with perspiration, her lips swollen from his ravaging kisses and her own teeth. "Oh God, don't stop, Ryan. Don't. You. Dare. Stop!"

He grunted and rose up on his knees, pushing her legs up higher against her chest. From this new position, he pounded into her at a deeper angle, his harsh groans mingling with her own as their flesh slapped noisily, his body taking her harder and faster than he'd ever fucked in his entire life. He was trapped by her, every deep thrust plowing the head of his cock past her cervix, pumping their bodies together in a need that went beyond the flesh, straight to the soul.

She'd read about this position so many times, never really getting what the big deal was. But she got it now. God, did she ever. The higher he pushed her legs, the further the thick heat of his cock dug into her, driving impossibly deeper with each powerful thrust. Her body stretched around him, somehow taking everything he gave her, until she knew nothing but the feel of him reshaping her limits—redefining the things she'd once known about herself.

They bucked. Strained. The bed slammed against the wall as their bodies went slick with heat, the sweat flying as their flesh slapped and sealed, fired with need. The silence of the morning was filled with the erotic sounds of skin and breath and hard, slippery wet fucking.

On a hammering downward stroke, Shea came again, if she'd ever stopped coming the first time, and Ryan felt his orgasm build from the bottom of his soul, surging forward, blinding him.

With a hoarse shout he poured himself into her, grinding himself against her, within her, hips to hips, cock to cunt. He filled her up until she was coated in his hot, sticky cum—drenched with his seed. He'd never get enough of it, shooting into her like that with no barriers between them. The searing, mind-blowing sensation seemed to turn him inside out and he ground his jaw down to keep from shouting.

When his limbs became too shaky to hold him, Ryan quickly lowered her legs and collapsed against her with a hard, heavy thud. Their breathing struggled in a ragged pattern as their battered lungs fought to draw sufficient air.

Against the sensitive column of her throat, Shea felt his whispered refrain of, "Oh God, Oh God, Oh God," but she could only smile in blissful, exhausted satisfaction. In the seconds that ticked by, the world went black, and she knew they'd either passed out or slept, unsure which it was...and too happy to care.

Chapter Eight

By the time they finally opened their eyes, it was late morning and the air conditioning vent was blowing cool air against their sleep-warmed skin. Ryan rumbled something about food on his way to the bathroom, so Shea forced her deliciously sore muscles to get out of bed and make the poor guy something to eat. Her stomach growled, and she realized she was pretty hungry herself.

It was amazing what hard, sweaty sex could do to a girl's appetite.

She'd just finished putting two warm, buttery flaked croissants on a plate for him when he strode into her tidy kitchen, looking rumpled and hungry and sexy as hell, wearing nothing but his faded jeans. Come to think of it, she was pretty damn hungry for him too. And she'd never noticed until this moment, with his big, hard, muscle-sculpted body crowding into the cramped space, just how tiny her cozy little kitchen really was. Not that this was a bad thing, she thought with an inner growl worthy of any female jungle cat, when it got him close and within easy licking distance.

Her carnal fantasies of picking up her honey bear and coating him up for a decadent treat were cut short, though, when he swallowed his last bite of croissant and said, "Let's spend the day together."

Yes, let's, she thought with a small smile, her stupid lovesick heart doing somersaults at the realization that he wasn't going to try and ditch her so quickly. She hadn't let herself think about what might be coming next, because she hadn't wanted to ruin her stolen moments of fun if he went back to being an obnoxious jerk and ignored her, pretending their early morning fuck-fest had never happened.

When she'd tried to tell him how she felt last night, he hadn't wanted to hear it, and so she'd held back all the things she'd been dying to say during the explosive moments she'd spent in his arms this morning. But waking up beside him had been so sweet, so perfect. A part of her—a really big part—had wanted to stay there forever, but she knew it'd be impossible to keep concealing the truth from him.

She was madly in love with Ryan McCall. The vibrant emotion was a living, breathing entity within her. It pulsed through her, around her, until she felt steeped in it. One look at her, and he should have been able to tell.

Unless it was the last thing in the world he wanted to see.

But he wanted to spend the day with her, which was too good to be true.

Or was it?

She looked at him over the rim of her favorite Van Gogh coffee mug and reminded herself that this guy, no matter how rough and rugged, was a hero at heart. "You're not babysitting me, are you?"

Those long-lashed, mesmerizing blue eyes of his narrowed at her tone; a small frown curving the edges of his sexy mouth. "What the hell does that mean?"

Shea shifted from foot to foot, feeling uncomfortably exposed in her short, terry robe, hair hanging wild around her face in a tumble of curls. But it wasn't her body that felt vulnerable, at least not right now. It was her stupid heart and its nagging insistence to get to the real meaning behind Ryan's attentions. "What I mean is—I know you talked to Hannah last night and I know she's probably worried about me, because she worries about everything." She blew a frustrated breath up through her curls, her gray eyes searching his, daring him to lie. "I just want to make sure Hannah didn't put you up to keeping an eye on me is all."

"I'm a big boy, Shea," he explained carefully, rubbing his rough hand against his even rougher, stubble-covered chin and jaw. It was a telling action—one he always did when he was thinking his way through a problem. And his problem was the little spitfire pinning him with her sparking gray gaze, as if she could see straight into him. The thought was unnerving as hell, because there were things in there he had no idea how to explain—things he didn't even want to put a name to.

Not yet.

How much of it was he willing to go out on a limb and reveal before she opened up and told him how she felt? Playing emotional chess had never been an issue for him before, because his emotions had always been carefully removed from his sexual encounters, but no way in hell was that the case with Shea. She had him so turned inside out, he didn't know which way was up anymore. All he knew was that he wanted her, and God help anyone who tried to take her away from him.

Knowing he had to say something, he drew a deep breath and took that first tentative step out on the limb. "As much as she'd like to, I don't let Hannah tell me what to do. And this isn't her idea. I asked because I want to spend time with you, and I thought it might be good for us to do something that doesn't involve fucking like bunnies—for at least part of the time."

She seemed to consider it for a moment. Then her rosy lips pursed and she said in that damn husky voice of hers, "But the fucking is so much fun."

The twinkle in her eyes told him she was teasing—but she was gonna get a hell of a lot more than "fun" if she wasn't careful. His dick apparently had no stopping power when it came to this woman.

She must've read his intent because she laughed, holding her hands up in front of her in mock surrender. "Okay, okay, what did you have in mind?"

Ryan shrugged his wide shoulders, the movement accentuating the breadth and muscles of his chest and arms. God help her. The man might not be pretty, but he was definitely testosterone based eye-candy, no two ways about it.

Leaning back against the counter with his big feet crossed at the ankles, he crossed his arms and said, "Why don't we grab coffee over at Borders so we can cruise the books, then take in that new Guy Ritchie flick, and make an early dinner reservation at that new Italian café, Vesuvio's, over in Buckhead?"

Well, as far as days went, Shea knew she could watch pig wrestling and still enjoy herself so long as she was with Ryan. But the day he'd just laid out sounded like heaven to her. Too good actually—and there was something a little too familiar about it.

Then it hit her. He'd just suggested they spend the day doing each of the things she'd previously asked him out to: coffee, the Ritchie flick, and dinner at Vesuvio's.

One slender black brow arched, her arms crossing as she mirrored his pose and leaned back against the opposite counter. "Come up with all of that on your own, did you?"

Moving away from the counter in a mouthwatering shift of powerful muscle and bone, he moved in on her, and her breath caught at the sexual power she could feel pumping off of him. He laced his fingers at the small of her back and then backed up so that the counter was once again at his back. He pulled her forward until she was standing between his legs, close enough that he could nibble on that sweet spot beneath her ear.

"Well," he drawled in that deep voice of his, flicking his tongue against her skin for a quick taste, "there is this beautiful, brazen, sassy babe who once asked me out to do just those things, and damn if I haven't been regretting saying no to her ever since."

Shea tried to rein in her heart, but the damn thing was tripping over itself in excitement. "So, um, now you're saying yes?"

"I think I'm saying a lot of things," he murmured huskily, and the sexy rasp shot straight to her melting cunt in a flash of heat.

"Yeah, well—I'm listening."

He grunted against the side of her throat, smiling at the tell-tale shiver that flowed through her whenever he licked her warm, sweet flesh. "Good. Why don't you tell me if you can figure out what I'm saying now?"

And suddenly he had one hand fisted in the curls at her nape, holding her head still as his mouth opened over hers and took delicious, instant possession. They bumped teeth, trying to get further within the other, and their tongues tangled in an erotic dance centered on taste and hunger. His other hand shoved up under the hem of her flimsy robe and went straight to her mound, cupping her wet pussy, teasing the ultra-sensitive flesh with the soft scrape of his calloused palm.

Ryan broke the kiss before he got too carried away, the sexy play of her tongue against his pumping him too hard, too fast. His teeth bit down gently on the lobe of her ear, and he gritted out in a dark, husky rasp, "What does this tell you, Shea?"

The heel of his hand ground down on her ripening, swelling clit as two fingers began to circle the puffy rim of her vulva, smearing the slippery juices round and round. Then he shot them deep, right up into the hot, tight core of her sex, and her back arched as she jerked into him, a raw cry ripping from her throat. "What does this tell you?" he grunted, working the thick fingers deeper, forcing the fist-tight channel to accept the feel of them. "What does it tell you when I finger-fuck you like this, and you know I'm imagining it's my cock I've got shoved up this hot cunt instead?"

"Uhhmm—" she groaned, her head back against her shoulders, eyes squeezed closed as she gave herself over to him completely. He loved how she did that—just utterly surrendered to wherever he wanted to take her—and he couldn't keep his hips from pushing into her, grinding the long, aching ridge of his cock into her hip.

"Come on, sugar," he drawled, pulling his fingers back to the edge of her hole, and then driving them deeper, his cock pounding behind his fly, demanding its turn to cram into the sweet little tunnel. "Come on and tell me what I'm saying."

Her hands gripped his naked shoulders, short nails biting into hard muscle, her head tossing from side to side.

"You want—you want to fuck me," she moaned, barely able to get the words out as the pleasure he pumped through her began to throb in her veins, burning her from the inside out. Her pussy was flooding, her juices soaking them both, and she wanted to scream at the incredible need building within—the aching demand to be packed full of his rigid cock and pounded into submission—forced to take everything he gave her.

"Good girl." Ryan rewarded her with the steady pressure of his thumb against her clit, its slow circular motion pulling shudder after shudder from her warm, sweet-scented body. The subtle scents of her cunt were filling the air as her juices flowed, and he found himself grinding his jaw against the blinding need to finish this right now, press her up against the refrigerator at his left, and pound the hell out of her until they were soaked in hot, sizzling cum and barely able to stand.

But the morning was both lazy and soft—and she was even softer in his arms. He didn't want to rush it. He wanted to savor every minute with her—every single intoxicating second. "Hell, you feel good wrapped around my fingers, you know that?"

"Uhhmm—"

His hand tightened in her curls again, pulling her face up to his with a gentle pressure despite its obvious strength. Against her lips, he rasped, "Yeah, I think you do. I'm beginning to think you know just what you do to me."

There was no way she could stop the slow, satisfied smile from spreading across her face. Lifting her heavy lids, she stared straight up into his glittering, smoldering blue stare. "I keep telling you, Ry, I can handle it."

The lines of his face were etched with hunger and a bone deep determination to remain this side of control. But she could see the pressure breaking him—could almost feel the craving dismantling his resolve.

Suddenly the two thick fingers inside of her were three, and with a change to the angle of his wrist, they were hitting her even higher...deeper. Her body responded with dizzying speed, growing warmer and wetter until the thick thrust of his fingers was making slurping sounds in her flesh.

"I love how you do that," he ground out, his voice gone hard and gravelly. "I love how you cream all over me when you get worked up. All I have to do is look at you and your hot little cunt starts going juicy."

His fingers slipped free, and she choked out some kind of hoarse demand, but then her breath was sucking in as his wet fingers began circling her clit, tweaking it, teasing it between his knuckles. She trembled in his arms, and her pussy spasmed in need, hungry for the delicious stretch of his cock, streaming with cream to make way for him. His fingers slipped lower, circling her slit again, teasing as they rubbed the moisture in dizzying circles.

"Ahhh...yeah. Feel that. You're so wet and sweet, Shea." His head lowered and his tongue licked at the sensitive shell of her ear, his voice a dark caress in the late morning sunlight. "That's it, honey. Drench this sweet thing with juices so I can lick them all up. I want to catch them on my tongue and swallow them down all sweet and warm. It's almost better than fucking you—eating this melting cunt right down my throat."

"Ryan," she moaned, unable to keep her hips from pressing against him, seeking fingers or cock or tongue.

Anything…*anything* that he could shove hard inside of her to make her come. "Please—"

"Shh," he rumbled, turning their bodies, his hand reaching back to the counter now behind her. "There's no rush this morning, Shea. I want to take my own sweet time and just suck and tongue this mouthwatering cunt until you're pounding against my face—screaming my name. Then I'm going to cram you full of cock again and make you come so hard you won't remember what it's like not to want this—not to fucking ache for this thing we have."

Before she could gasp, he had her pushed up on the counter, the cold Formica shocking against her bare ass, and was calling on all of his sexual experience to push her to the edge. His fingers pumped into her, over and over, while his thumb worked her pulsing clit like a trigger. She writhed and trembled in his arms, and then she was gasping for air, a harsh cry breaking past her lips as her muscles clenched, held on that painful precipice, and then clenched tighter with tension as the impending orgasm began gaining intensity, her body squeezing sharply like a wire getting ready to snap.

She was nearly there when he pulled back, and she wanted to scream with frustration as she watched him move away, grabbing something from the counter behind him. Within seconds he'd turned back to her, his hand moving quickly between her legs before she could see what he held—but she knew as soon as she felt the nozzle moving purposefully between the puffy lips of her pleading, weeping sex.

God bless him, the man had obviously been having his own wicked fantasies about that honey bear, and he was more than ready to follow through on them. The sweet, sticky substance oozed up into her, warm and thick, mixing with her own slick fluids. Ryan bent down and put his talented tongue to good use—exceptional use, actually—working the honey up into her, sending it deeper and deeper with each eating stroke. An uncontrollable quake took hold of her core, slowly spreading out through her extremities until she was a trembling, quivering mass of hunger and need.

"Oh fuck...*fuck*," she groaned, nearly panicking at the strange sensation of falling away from reality. She was tumbling headfirst into pure orgasmic bliss, and Ryan was the sinful devil propelling her straight over the edge, forcing her higher and higher, only to make the eventual tumble that much more exhilarating.

Another squeeze of his powerful fingers and her cunt flooded with hot cream and golden honey, creating a carnal feast for his lips and searching tongue. Then his hand moved lower, and it was with a jolting, shocking bolt of recognition that she realized he was inserting the small nozzle into the tight rim of her ass.

"Oh my God—what are you—"

"Shh," he murmured against the swollen lips of her pussy, giving her a gentle, laving kiss, like a sweetheart's gift. "Relax and let me, Shea. Don't fight it. It'll feel so fucking good, I promise."

Her hands found his shoulders, ready to shove him away. "I can't...I've never—"

"Trust me," he drawled, catching the pulsing bud of her clit between his teeth and sucking with a strong, sensuous swirling of lips and tongue. He didn't relent until her fingers were curling back into him, her short nails biting into his muscle and flesh.

Another squeeze of his fingers and the soft, oozing honey plunged into her ass, the small nozzle feeling uncomfortably good, buried there in the tight little hole that she'd never considered exploring sexually. She'd never realized it would feel so good—strange, yes, but undeniably...scandalously thrilling—to be penetrated there while his mouth worked a sensual magic on her clit.

And then his head was shifting, her throbbing clit left swollen and sensitized, and she arched her hips, desperate to regain the mind-blowing contact so she could come. But Ryan had other ideas, and before she'd even guessed his intention, she felt the warm, outrageously wicked slide of his tongue around the buried nozzle of her honey bear.

"Oh God...wait...what—"

"Mmm," he groaned, his hot breath brushing against her trembling flesh. "Don't tell me no, Shea. Just let me show you good it can feel—how fucking hot you make me."

The nozzle slipped free, and heaven help her, he replaced it with the hot slide of his tongue, twirling it just inside the honey-coated pucker of her ass. "Ahhhh," she cried out, the raw, pleasure-filled wail like a rape of sound in the gentle quiet of her kitchen—but she couldn't hold it in, nor the sharp, "Oh God!" that quickly followed in its echo.

His fingers bit into her hips, holding her steady at the edge of the counter, while his tongue took possession in a carnal kiss of strange, forbidden ecstasy. She could feel the steady, shallow plunge and glide inside her ass, the sexy stubble of his cheeks rubbing against her naked cheeks, the soft rasp of his hair against her spread thighs.

His tongue stroked the ultra-sensitive rim, and a wave of heat spread over the surface of her skin in a warm, moist flush. Her blood seemed thicker, heart working double-time to pump it through her veins, lungs laboring to draw a sufficient breath. Her pussy gushed, open and grasping for something to bear down on, and she nearly fainted when he shoved her hungry slit full of three thick fingers, his tongue slipping free to greedily lick the remaining honey and streaming rivulets of sex juice from her skin.

She shouted hoarsely, hips pumping, as the deliciously narrow channel suctioned tight around his fingers, and he groaned in triumph, grunting, "That's it, baby. Shit, you feel so good. Just keep pumping my fingers for more. I want to feel you come."

She jerked in his arms, groaning a low, dark cry of sound, and then she was coming — hard and fast and strong — drenching and squeezing the hell out of him.

Ryan growled and immediately withdrew his fingers with a wet sound of resistance, only to lower his head for another deep dig with his tongue, thrusting it straight up the flushed, pumping mouth of her pussy. His mouth filled with her cum, and God help him, it was even better than her juices. Hotter, creamier, and he sucked it down his throat with greedy satisfaction, knowing it was a taste he'd crave for the rest of his life. No other would ever do again, because no other flavor had ever tasted like *his* — as if she were his very own — made just for him.

And now that his tongue had feasted on that sweet, honey-and-cum coated flesh, his cock was angrily demanding its own turn to fuck.

His jeans were ripped open and his massive cock crammed into her, all the way to his balls within the mere space of seconds. She was still coming, her nails struggling for a hold on the slick surface of his shoulders. The force of pleasure that rocked down the core of his cock at being buried deep inside her convulsing sheath nearly buckled his knees.

Unable to hold himself still while she adjusted to him, Ryan carefully drew himself out of her—a low, rumbling sound surging from his chest at the way her pussy grasped to hold on to the long length of him. When only the tip remained within, she raised her shoulders so that together they looked down to see him poised at her entrance. He gleamed wetly, impossibly thick, the veined skin of his cock flushed and slick with her cream.

A tremor shook his entire body as their eyes reconnected, and then he rammed himself back into her, grinding his hips against hers, completely lost to the wonder of her delectable cunt surrounding him. He'd had sex thousands of times, with more women than he could remember, but he'd never felt anything like this. Fucking Shea was so new and novel and intense, he felt as if he were the one with so little friggin' experience.

Then she pulled him to her and bit his honey-and-cream covered lip between her strong, white teeth, and he fucking lost it.

With his hips pounding his cock into her, he spread the lips of her pussy wider, making it easier to watch the way her tiny slit swallowed him whole, sucking him in with the slippery sounds of flesh and fluids.

Wanting to share the erotic view, Shea braced her hands on the counter behind her and leaned forward. Then they were both watching the delicious sight of his long, thick cock stretching her tender opening wide, so wide, plowing into her with more and more force, giving her everything he had.

"It's so good…it's so good…it's so good," he gritted through his teeth over and over, and she couldn't help but agree. It was mind-shattering, the warmth of pleasure flowing through her, the overwhelming sensations screaming down her nerve endings.

His big hands bit into her hips, holding her hard so that he could pound into her even harder, working her on his cock, their flesh slapping together in the soft quiet of the morning. Shea dug her heels into the small of his back, pumping herself against him as they struggled for control, their bodies going slick with sweat and heat, fired by an arcing, aching need.

Ryan's hand snaked up her spine, snagging her curls, and then he pulled back until her sweet, bouncing breasts were thrust in his face. Her back arched and his mouth closed over one soft mound like a dark, wet fire that burned with pleasure. He laved at the puffy pink nipple, and then drew in the entire breast, suckling her with rhythmic tugs that came all the way from his throat. The delicious pull shot to her womb, clenching her tighter, pulling him deeper into her until she'd taken every incredible inch.

He filled her up so full she felt ready to burst open—shattering around him—but her pussy only held him stronger, pushed him to drive up higher, deeper, forcing that cock harder and harder into her core.

"How in the hell do you feel better every time I get inside of you?" he grated, each word timed with the pulsing jab of his hips—the thick, powerful ramming of his cock into her wet, clinging depths. "Every single time, you just get better and better."

The rough words pushed her up the cliff, and she went rushing over, her muscles clenching so tightly on his throbbing shaft that he ground his mouth down on hers, shouting into the warm, wet cavern. He swallowed her screams with savage intent while her pussy pulled him in like a suction, and then he was growling into her mouth as his orgasm exploded and his hot cum spurted up into her in a hard, vicious stream, jerking out of his cock.

When they were spent and sated, Shea collapsed back onto the counter, Ryan's big body following her down, his golden head resting against the soft, heaving swell of her chest.

She waited until her breathing finally evened out and she was able to draw enough air to speak, then lifted her hand and sifted her fingers through the soft silk of his hair. She laughed softly, her mind still spinning in the afterglow. "I guess you really are saying yes, then."

Ryan lifted his head and stared into her smoky eyes with such raw possession it made her breath catch. Then his mouth closed over hers once more, so warm and delicious and sweet, she just wanted to flow into him.

"Yeah," he rumbled, taking the fullness of her bottom lip between his teeth and tugging gently until she opened wider for the decadent plunge of his tongue. "Now I'm saying yes."

Chapter Nine

After the hot and heavy, mind-blowing session in the kitchen, Ryan put in a call to maintenance about her front door and then made arrangements to have Spalding's piece of shit pickup impounded. Then he ran back over to his apartment for a quick change of clothes while Shea went to get herself ready for the most exciting day of her life.

She was nervous and shaky and so giddy she felt ridiculous, but it wasn't every day that a woman got to go on a dream date with her fantasy man. She thought it might even be better than sex, having him all to herself, taking the time to talk and get to know each other, sharing a romantic candlelit dinner.

Almost. But not quite. There couldn't be anything in the world better than having Ryan driving deep inside her body, pounding her open—but a dream date definitely qualified as a close second. The only thing that could top the sex would be for him to tell her he loved her—and she *sooo* wasn't going to think about that right now.

Oh, she still wanted it, but she wasn't going to let her heart screw this up by letting it rule her actions. She was going to have fun and enjoy herself, and that's just what she did.

They drank down tall, ice-frothed coffees topped with whipped cream and caramel while weaving their way through the book-lined aisles at Borders, pausing along the way to discuss their favorite authors. Not that she'd ever thought he wasn't academic or anything—in fact, she thought he was probably one of the sharpest people she'd ever known—but she was taken by surprise by how well-read he actually was. Somehow she'd just never imagined he had much time for reading between his very demanding career and overly active sex life, but he proved her wrong by discussing many of the mainstream, bestselling authors, and even some of the more obscure writers who were just beginning to make a name for themselves.

And what was truly amazing was that the more she got to know him, the harder she fell. The love that had been growing inside of her for the last three months began to blossom like a bud exposed to showers and sunshine, and suddenly it was taking on a vibrant life of its own. But if he saw the evidence burning in her eyes, he didn't let on, so Shea struggled to tamp it down and keep it locked up tight before it spilled out and she couldn't ever pull it back in.

Of course, he didn't make it easy. Especially when he grabbed her in the deserted back fiction aisle, wrapping her body within the strong, deliciously muscled circle of his arms. One second they were softly laughing at something he'd said and she turned to smile at him—then, in the next, she was captured between his gorgeous body and the rows full of Vonnegut and Voltaire at her back.

She looked up at him with a startled, excited expression on her face, not really knowing what to expect. He'd never touched her with anything other than a sexual intent, and somehow she knew that he wasn't looking for the thrill of getting caught screwing in the back aisle of a bookstore, tumbling copies of *Cat's Cradle* and *Candide* at their feet.

No...this time it was different. The dark look in his heavy-lidded gaze was no less hungry, but this time there was more to it. A deeper emotion. An underlying tenderness. A soft, aching need for connection that struck her harder than anything else that had happened between them to this point. A vulnerability that she'd never in a million lifetimes have thought she would see on this man's face. The fact that it was all for her only made it that much more wrenchingly special.

Ryan read the question in her eyes, his own crinkling at the corners as he tried to laugh off his intense, uncharacteristic loss of control. "I just need to kiss you," he murmured softly...roughly, his face already lowering to hers, big hands pressing against the slender line of her back, pulling her into his wide, tall frame while he pushed her harder against the book-lined wall. "I just need the touch of your lips...your taste in my mouth," he rasped, voice thick with wonder. "I don't know how you fucking do this to me, but I'm dying for it like some junked out addict."

"Oh God," she whispered, his words killing her with the need to have him—everything he was—forever. To grab hold of him and keep him as her own for every day and night for the rest of her life. And then his warm, silk-textured lips touched hers, and every thought fled her mind as rapidly as they'd been born. Love rushed up through her in a pure, wondrous burst of perfect, spellbinding heat and she fell into him, weightless, flying purely on sensation.

It was Shea who made the first aggression, whose tongue stroked invitingly across the sensual line of his mouth until he opened to let her in. A low, dangerous growl freed itself from her throat, burrowing into her belly where it curled around itself and snuggled in for a slow, deep burn. An aching hunger that would only grow stronger, awaiting its turn to feast and gorge on pleasure in a greedy, rapacious feeding.

"You are so damn dangerous," he grunted. His big, trembling hands found the warm cheeks of her face, holding them as if in prayer, while his mouth worshipped hers with more longing than she'd ever dreamed she could endure. The long, massive ridge of his jeans-covered cock pressed against her mound, spearing her with need, and she cried into his mouth, the raw sound swallowed by his.

Suddenly his head was angling from one side to the other, his tongue invading deeper, investigating every recess of her mouth, claiming possession, ownership, while he held her face immobile, keeping her utterly at his mercy. The dynamic shifted, and what started out as a gentle exploration erupted into a full-fledged devouring of sweetly erotic tastes and flavors—no longer a kiss, but an intimate eating of one mouth into another.

Shea sobbed and clawed to get closer, mindless to everything, including her surroundings, as she struggled to get her hands wedged down the front of his jeans, wanting the immediate hot, hard feel of his cock.

She reached gold—rock-hard and pulsing with power—just as his rough palms skimmed down her thighs, collecting fistfuls of skirt. Then they were sliding up smooth, naked skin, her skirt pooling over his forearms, as her thighs parted eagerly, swollen cunt starving for his touch. Calloused fingertips skimmed through her wet, slippery lips, and another growl crawled into her mouth, sliding down her throat.

"Uhhmm," she moaned, hips arching as two wicked fingers found her silky slit and drove deep. They were long and thick, perfect for a delicious, dizzying finger-fuck, as they began thrusting into her, curving forward until the rough tips were hitting her little hot spot, sending her dangerously close to climax. Her hips pumped, forcing her drenched, clinging flesh down on those thick digits, her small hand squeezing tighter, relishing the feel of his throbbing cock in her grip.

She was just on the verge of exploding when he wrenched his mouth from hers and grunted, "Shit. We can't do this here. I'm about two seconds away from fucking you without giving a crap who can see, and I don't wanna embarrass you like that."

Two seconds more and she would have told him she didn't give a damn, to get on with it already, but they both heard the shocked gasp and low male grunt at just that moment. Their heads turned slowly, in perfect unison, to see the attractive, twenty-something couple standing at the end of the aisle. The woman's brown eyes were round, shocked wide with disapproval, while the man's stayed glued to the erotic sight of Ryan's hand shoved inside the leg of her thong, fingers buried up her pulsing cunt.

A violent wave of possession struck him out of nowhere, and before he could claw his way to the surface of sanity, Ryan felt the burning jealousy take hold. It sucked him deeper into that dark, hidden place where everything he felt for this woman churned with the need to break free. He knew he should pull his hand out from between her legs, get her own talented little hand out of his damn pants, and get her the hell outta there before he sank even further, but he did none of those things.

What he did was unlike anything he'd ever done before—not even in the carelessness of youth. Knowing she watched the fascinated couple with stunned eyes,

Ryan lowered his mouth to her ear, his fingers resuming their thick plunge and stroke inside the sopping, delectable heat of her juice-soaked cunt.

She shuddered in his arms, her entire body going stiff with tension, wondering what the hell he was doing. "Ry-Ryan…?"

Her long skirt flowed over his powerful arms, and he wrenched the material to the side with his free hand, wanting there to be no doubt as to where his fingers were buried. "You see the way he's watching you?" he growled, fingers pumping harder…faster…until they were making slick, slurping sounds over the gentle music of the store. "He's watching the way my fingers are drilling you— fucking you—and wishing like hell they were his own. Wishing it was his tongue shoved up inside of you. His cock."

And it was true. She could see it—feel it—watching the way the stranger's eyes remained riveted on the pink, plump flesh between her trembling thighs. She could feel how badly he wanted it to be his own hand shoved between her drenched folds, crammed into her open sex, furiously pumping her for pleasure.

"What are you doing?" she whispered. Her voice sounded thick with disbelief and the strange, unbearable arousal she couldn't disguise.

"Hell if I know—but I want you to come," he ordered roughly, fingers moving faster, muscles and veins sticking out in his thick forearm as he worked her, ruthless in his intent. His dark, hooded eyes cut back to the couple. The guy's baby blues were glazed with lust, his pants tenting with his too obvious erection, and Ryan wanted to howl at the moon from the feral, primitive impulse to stake his claim on Shea right there and then, forcing the guy to watch it.

"Let's show the little bastard how hard you come for me," he grunted, knowing the couple could hear him, wanting them to know she was his to do with as he pleased, however he pleased—needing them to know how completely he controlled her sexuality. At that moment he'd have fucked her in front of the whole fucking town just to prove the undeniable fact that she was his to fuck in whatever way he chose.

His—and no other's.

The strange, uncomfortable, somehow exhilarating eroticism of the moment washed over her, crashing down on her, and suddenly Shea was gritting her teeth to choke back a guttural scream of release as her pussy spasmed, clamping down hard, and then began the steady pump and grind of orgasm that had her creaming all over him, soaking his hand. "Oh God," she sobbed, watching the strangers watch her, while Ryan took her right where he wanted, his wicked fingers keeping her going until the pumping of her hips slowly eased and her pussy felt raw from the unforgiving force of sensation. "*God.*"

She could feel the hot color burning in her cheeks, whether from coming or being watched by strangers while she did, she couldn't say. Probably a bit of both. The woman's wide eyes darted back and forth between her shocked, pleasure-filled expression and Ryan's fierce, possessive scowl, but the guy's hot gaze stayed glued right on her crotch. Time moved slowly, sluggishly, weighted with tension, making it difficult to breathe. Just when she was certain they'd turn around and run to find the nearest manager to lodge a complaint—or better yet, race home for a fast, furious quickie—the guy let out an audible groan and licked his lips.

She had about a second to think, "Oh…hell," and then Ryan's fingers slipped from between her legs with a soft, yet audibly wet suction. Caught between dizzying shock at their display of exhibitionism and the uncomfortable realization that it had aroused the hell out of her to be so publicly claimed, Shea wrenched her eyes away from the young stud to see Ryan lift his cum-soaked fingers to his mouth. A small, strangled yelp stuck in her throat as his tongue snaked out to take a long, sexy, clearly enjoyable lick of the glistening juice shimmering on his skin.

"Fuck me," the guy groaned, grabbing his cock through his jeans while his wife or girlfriend or whoever the hell she was stared at Ryan with equal parts distress and dazed desire.

He took another long, sensuous lick of creamy cum, and then said in a low, rough voice. "Show's over, asshole. Now get lost."

The woman jumped, startled by the undisguised threat of violence in his tone, and quickly pushed the still stunned man back around the corner.

Suddenly they were alone, and Shea didn't have a clue what to say.

Ryan shifted, helping her to remove her death grip on his cock, and then they were staring helplessly at each other. She stared down at her hand with a surprised look of recollection, as if she'd only just realized she'd had it in his pants the entire time the voyeuristic couple had been looking on.

"Ah…shit," he sighed, raking one hand through his hair in a boyish gesture that tugged at her heart every damn time he did it. "I'm...ah," he stumbled awkwardly, looking almost sheepish as a slow flush worked its way into his gold-stubbled cheeks. "Ah hell," he drawled. "I didn't mean to do that like...that...in this place. I don't know what the hell I was thinking, doing that to you."

Shea shifted restlessly from foot to foot, not a clue how to react or what to say. Finally, she managed to mumble out a, "Do you think we need to, um, worry about the police? I don't want to end up on one of those *When Good Girls Go Bad* videos or anything."

The sensual line of his mouth cocked up at one corner in a teasing grin, blue eyes sparkling with mischief...and an underlying, undeniable satisfaction that he couldn't hide. He'd thrown her headfirst into a mind-shattering orgasm that had left his hand feeling bruised and his heart aching from the need to claim her for good...for his own...forever.

He tapped the tip of her nose with his finger, relieved she wasn't ripping into him for his crazy-assed caveman routine, but not about to blame her if she did. "Nah, you don't have to worry about any of that. Take a look around. There aren't any cameras on this aisle."

Instead of checking out their surroundings, she stared fixedly at his chin. "And the police?" she asked with a sick feeling churning in the pit of her stomach, suddenly wondering about how she'd manage to explain to the university about being arrested for lewd public conduct. Talk about freaking embarrassing.

"Ah sugar, I am the police, remember?"

"Oh, yeah...okay."

His hand hooked under her chin, lifting her face, and their gazes reconnected with an exhilaratingly, tingling burst of emotion. Before they even knew it was happening, or could explain why, they were smiling at one another, eyes shining with mischievous delight. Then smiles quickly turned to grins, grins to soft chuckles, and within moments, they were laughing so hard tears were streaming down their cheeks, their sides aching with stitches.

Shea was still giggling like crazy when Ryan ushered her through the front of the store, thankfully without running into any outraged managers or law enforcement officers. They climbed up into his truck, wiping their eyes as they tried to get their laughter under control, only to crack up again every time they looked at each other.

Leaning over the console, Ryan planted a soft, lingering kiss against her smiling lips. "Thanks for not getting pissed at me."

"And thanks—" she stuttered, eyes bright with devilish humor as she suddenly began hiccupping. "Thanks for making me come."

"My pleasure," he growled, nipping at her lip just as she hiccupped again. Then they were dissolving into another helpless round of laughter, arms clutched around their aching stomachs as they tried to hold it in.

"Ah shit," he finally drawled, resting his forehead against her still shaking shoulder. "We must be crazy."

"Well, if it makes you feel any better," she hiccupped, unable to resist the temptation to run her fingers through his silk-textured scrub of hair, his warm, masculine scent filling her lungs, "I've never had so much fun shopping for books in my entire life."

His head lifted, a lopsided grin pulling up one corner of his mouth. "Yeah, me neither," he laughed softly, but the look in his dark blue eyes was once again tender, shooting straight through her, like an invisible claw spearing into her chest, squeezing her heart. She stared at him, knowing that everything she felt was right there for him to see—and no longer giving a damn.

His gaze moved over every feature, every detail of her face, with an intense look of longing, and then settled back on her eyes. "Since I promised myself I wouldn't fuck you again until tonight—"

"Why?" she interrupted, lost in her own exploration, mesmerized by the rugged growth of golden-stubble on his cheeks, the strong line of his cheekbones and the sexy, slightly crooked line of his nose, as if it'd been broken and reset at some point in his life.

He caught a curl and tucked it gently behind her ear, then trailed his fingers along the delicate curve of her jaw, marveling at the softness of her skin. She didn't normally wear makeup, other than the slick rub of gloss on her lips, and he loved the bare, natural feel of her flesh beneath his fingertips. "'Cause you need some rest for what I've got planned for you later on."

"Oh…"

"Yeah. A lot of rest. So you wanna go catch the flick?"

Was it suddenly warmer in the truck, or was she on the verge of spontaneous combustion just from the searing look of heat and sexual promise burning in his beautiful blue eyes? She swallowed thickly, trying not to pant. "Uh, yeah, sure. The movie sounds great."

So after books, coffee, and their mild stint at exhibitionism, they hit the theater, and Shea found the Ritchie movie as fun as his other crazy London mob-scene tales. Ryan hadn't caught his previous films, but he laughed right along with her and casually suggested they rent his earlier stuff to watch together. Once again, her heart went into overdrive, and she figured at this rate she was going to have to either distract herself with more mind-blowing sex, which made thinking a near impossibility, or simply cave in.

Since breaking down and pouring her heart out would probably be a surefire way to get rid of him for good—when all she really wanted to do was keep him forever—it was an enormous relief when the next opportunity for sex finally presented itself.

Their dinner at Vesuvio's was as mouthwatering as the Lifestyle review had claimed it would be, and the atmosphere proved to be a perfect ending to their day. They talked about his work, her thesis, and her student teaching at the university. He shared funny stories about growing up with Hannah and how he'd met Derek on a stakeout turned disaster. They laughed, talked, and learned, to their mutual surprise, that they had a hell of a lot more in common than they'd ever imagined.

She'd been determined not to worry about all those things she couldn't control—from her heart and his intentions, to the nightmare last night with Spalding—and had ended up having the best damn day of her life.

Throughout the afternoon, Ryan had been off and on the phone with Derek, learning some surprising information. It'd turned out that Spalding had several outstanding warrants from three different states. His bastard ass was going to be put away for a good long while, and she wasn't going to waste her time with Ryan worrying about the jerk.

In fact, the only thing she was starting to worry about was how much longer she was going to have to wait to feel Ryan inside of her again. She needed him to ease the ache that had been steadily gaining intensity since she'd last held him buried deep within her body—and she needed him now.

Looking at him over the rim of her wineglass, the rich merlot slipping smoothly down her throat, Shea felt her empty pussy grow warm and wet at the delicious sight he made sitting across from her. His short, golden hair tossed from the wind, his blue eyes dark in the candlelight, and his mouth twisted into the kind of smile that said he knew she was watching him, and that she more than liked what she saw.

Setting down his fork, he leaned back in his chair and gave her a very direct stare—one that said he more than liked her looks as well. Her nipples tightened beneath her soft camisole top, pressing against the light cotton, and he stared at them until she began to shiver, before raising his hot gaze back to hers.

"What are you thinking about?" he asked in a low, rough rumble.

Shea set her glass back on the table, running her finger thoughtfully around the rim, wondering where this was all going to lead to tonight, and not really caring so long as he fucked her before she went out of her mind. More heat gathered down low, making her swell in preparation, going warm and slick. The need was so sharp—it was a struggle not to wiggle around in her chair. "What are *you* thinking about?"

Her eyes moved casually over the restaurant, and Ryan leaned back in his chair, a lazy grin of anticipation spreading across his ruggedly chiseled features, waiting for her gaze to meet his again. When it did, he smiled. "I'm thinking that if you keep looking at me like you're thinking about having this hard-on I'm sporting under the table for dessert, you'll find yourself laid out over it with your skirt over your head, and I'll be fucking that tight little cunt of yours before you know what hit you."

Oh, um, yes please!

She trailed her fingers across the gleaming wooden surface, touching her tongue to the sensual curve of her upper lip. "You know, I've got a table almost like this at home."

His gaze narrowed, smoldering blue eyes full of desire. "Then what the hell are we waiting for? Let's go break it in."

As they waited for the valet to bring his truck around, Ryan kept her within the possessive circle of his arm, snuggled up against his side, uncomfortably aware of the attention she drew. She'd caught the eye of nearly every man in the restaurant as they made their way out, and the two young valets huddled behind their podium had been damn near drooling over her ever since they walked out into the sweet, balmy air of the early evening.

It wasn't that she was the most beautiful woman there—though in his eyes, no other woman could compare to her. No, it was the way she glowed. Shea sparkled with life—like a bubbling current of energy that flowed through her, intoxicating everyone who came into contact with it. It was there in the mischievous gleam in her gray eyes, the alluring lift of her lips, the sensuous lines of her body. It was in the touch of her fingertips against his skin, as if he could feel the current pulsing through her. It was visible in the playful bounce of her rich, satiny curls, so soft and luxurious, and in the sexy lilt of her husky voice.

And, damn it, he wanted to claim it all as his own.

All of it.

All of her.

He wasn't used to the odd, prickling burn in his stomach, the unpleasant taste of jealousy burning on his tongue, and he sure as hell didn't care for it. He'd never felt this incessant, insane need for possession over another human being—the need to hold her close and keep her there, battling against anyone or anything that threatened to take her away. Derek had jokingly called him a caveman and that's what he felt like. As immature as it was, he was ready to beat his chest and swing his club, challenging all to accept his ownership.

Hell, where had the laid back, easygoing, fuck-for-fuck's sake guy gone? The one who'd inhabited his body for as long as he could remember. Who had been burned once and now kept women at a comfortable distance—like the dog who'd been struck by a car and now knew better than to get too close to one again.

Whatever feelings he'd had as a young man in the throes of his first serious love—or lust, as it were—shit, that was nothing compared to this. It was like comparing the morning sun and the midnight sky, as different as night and day. One had been about pride and immature ego, while the other was about necessity.

Yeah, necessity. Hunger. Need. And beneath it all, something deeper.

And no way in hell was he going there to find out what it was.

Christ, he was having a hard enough time dealing with the emotions he could already put a name to.

They made the drive home in record time, with Shea gripping her door handle until her knuckles turned white as Ryan sped through the maze of surface streets. Obviously she'd provoked him, and now she couldn't help but feel she had a tiger by the tail. Of course, she was looking forward to letting him go, wondering how she could keep finding the idea of sleeping with him more exciting each and every time. Apparently this kind of need didn't diminish with experience — or maybe it was just that Ryan was all the provocation she'd ever need.

When he cut the engine on his big four-wheel drive GMC, she opened her door and stepped down on shaky legs before he could get around to her, so he wasted no time, simply grabbing hold of her small hand and dragging her along behind him. Together they made the short walk down the narrow sidewalk, past his apartment and on around the corner to hers. Her keys were taken from her hand, her now repaired door opened, closed, and then she was being pressed against the solid wooden surface, Ryan's rigid body at her front.

He sank his teeth into the side of her neck — not hard enough to hurt, just to tantalize — then stroked his tongue over the light mark. "Take your panties off."

She tried to say okay, but hey, it was difficult to talk when your breath was panting and your heart was threatening to hammer through your chest. Luckily her body was already saying everything that needed to be said. She shifted, reaching beneath the hem of her skirt, and pulled until they fell to her ankles.

Black lace again, he saw with hot eyes, and he bent down to take them off, lifting first one ankle and then the other. Looking up at her, he lifted them to his face and breathed deeply, a gruff noise growling low in his throat.

As if there was nothing unusual about it, he folded them up and placed them in his pocket, then wrapped his big, hard hands around her slender ankles, sliding them up her thighs, until he stopped just short of touching her pussy. She was already so wet, the insides of her thighs were sticky with cream, and he knew it. The second his fingertips touched her slick juices, he smiled, rubbing them in with a massaging motion that worked her warm cream into her heated skin. Then he spoke, and his deep drawl was rough with lust and longing. "You're dripping for me, Shea, and all I've done is touch you." Her mouth opened, but no sound escaped, just her breath rushing hard and fast as she stared down at him.

"Did you know you taste even sweeter than you smell?" Without waiting for an answer, not really expecting one, he leaned forward, nuzzling her mound through the thin cotton of her skirt. Her scent was deeper here, making his mouth water, and he wanted to devour her, raking her with tongue and teeth and lips until she screamed herself blue. Then he'd give her a fucking hard enough to make her understand that this all meant a hell of a lot more than a weekend fling.

Nuzzling her, driving them both insane by taking it slow after his mad desperation to get her here, he kissed her cunt through cotton. He licked it, his tongue pushing between her naked folds beneath the insubstantial barrier of cloth, and soft little sounds began escaping her throat.

Opening his mouth, he bit through the wet material—the fabric drenched from both his kiss and her fluids—and held the front of her mound in his teeth. It was a primitive instinct, like a wolf biting into the neck of its mate, showing her exactly who she belonged to. She was going to get everything she'd asked for—and a hell of a lot more.

Holding her in his teeth, breathing in her rich, earthy scent, all he wanted was to take her like an animal, hard and savage and pounding, again and again.

The instant he felt her hands sift through his hair, holding him to her, he released his hold, nuzzling deeper, his tongue reaching further into the cloth-covered cleft of the sweetest pussy he'd ever had.

"God," she groaned above him, her eyes so big they nearly swallowed her face. "Is this normal?"

He pulled back only far enough to speak, making sure she could still feel the warmth of his breath through her skirt. He knew she was talking about their violent physical connection, the sex so hot it nearly left them singed, and he thought she just might be asking about his penchant for going down on her too. "It isn't normal for me, no," he murmured, choosing to address the second issue. He leaned forward to press a kiss against her navel, the silver loop just visible beneath the bottom of her camisole blouse. "Must be you. What can I say? You're addictive."

"I am?"

"Yeah, you are. Once I got my first taste of you, I was hooked. Now I can't get enough. You got a problem with that?"

The sparkle was back in her eyes, warning him he was about to be sassed again. "No, no problem," she quipped. "But just to be sure it's really me—maybe I should conduct a taste test or something?"

He fought back a sudden smile. "What? Like the Pepsi Challenge, only guys get to taste you instead?"

She traced the outline of his lips with one fingertip, dipping just inside to press against his tongue. "Yeah. What do you think?"

Ryan bit down gently on the slender digit in his mouth, soothing the sting with a slow swirl of his tongue until her eyes went vague above him. Letting it slip free, his lips lifted in a warm, sinister smile. "I think that little shit in the bookstore today was all but drooling for a chance to get his tongue up this sweet little cunt," he drawled, "but I should probably warn you that I'll kill any bastard who ever tries to lay a hand on you, much less a tongue."

He rose before her, towering over her by the time he was done, then gripped her ass in his hands and hauled her up against the front of his very hard, very aroused body. "And I should also probably warn you that your teasing just earned you the hardest, rawest fuck of your life."

And he wasn't kidding. Before she could think of anything witty to say, she found herself perched on the edge of her table and any clothes she'd been wearing or thoughts that they'd ever be suitable to wear again were long gone as Ryan shredded them from her body by gripping handfuls of delicate fabric and wrenching. Within seconds she was naked and wet and panting, and that's all the notice she had before he ripped open his fly and his massive cock was rising high into the air between them, and then even higher inside of her.

He found her quivering opening with unerring skill and drove himself to the hilt with the first plunge, a deliberately brutal flesh through flesh kind of thrust, forcing her body to take him to the root. One hand fisted in her hair, the other gripped her ass, angling her where he wanted, and then he began a hard, fast, steady rhythm that had him pounding every thick inch of his cock into her. Over and over and over, he pushed the erotic pleasure of it through her until she thought it would start seeping out from her pores. She was at her limit, as full as she could get, and yet he just kept going, cramming it in—until she lost all sense of boundaries and angles and could feel nothing but the ramming thrusts of his cock into her cunt, pushing the pulse of his heartbeat into the back of her throat.

Her mouth was open, her eyes trapped by his, her body jarring to the pounding rhythm, making the table screech across the tile beneath its legs. The flush on her cheeks spread down her neck to cover her naked breasts, and when he felt the first clench of her womb, his lips pulled back, showing his straight, white teeth. He bent her over until the cool, polished surface of the table was at her back, his still clothed body at her front, and the massive shaft of his cock a ruthless, hammering force of pleasure between her legs.

Ryan looked down at her—and wanted more. Gripping the backs of her knees, he pulled them up and out, pushing them flat at her sides, and her pussy spread wide open. Ah yeah, that was better. Her cunt pulled open, pink and pearly, while his cock rammed in and out of the delicate hole, stretching the tender flesh to its limit. It was a savage, ruthless possession—just as he'd promised—brutal in its intensity.

Shea writhed beneath him, back arching as he lowered his head to one ripe nipple. His lips opened to suck her deep, working the tiny bud against the roof of his mouth, and she exploded in a rush so powerful it was almost more pain than pleasure. She jolted and jerked and shouted—marveling at how something that felt so good could feel almost like death.

When she could draw breath once again, she wrapped her arms around his still hammering body and hugged him tight as he rested his head between her breasts and came in a long, scalding stream, jetting into her until he could feel the climax raking down his nerve endings, scraping him raw. His jaw ached as he ground it down— his body shuddering hard as he pumped hot spurts of cum deep into her welcoming cunt. He'd never felt anything so painfully sweet as those full bursts of seed erupting from the head of his cock.

Holy shit. She'd killed him. That was it. Nothing was left but a wreck of a man as he collapsed against her, smiling at her breathless grunt as she got pressed under his weight. God, she was so cute.

Her small hands were coasting down his back, stroking him like a pet, and he knew with an absolute certainty that reached his soul that he'd never find anything better than being in her arms, his cock wrapped up tight in her body. Damn, it just didn't get any better than that.

"Remind me—" she murmured against the top of his head when she was finally able to draw enough air for speech again. "Remind me to do that more often."

"Do what?"

"Make you jealous," she said with a very satisfied smile in her voice.

"Then I gotta warn you—I might not be so gentle next time."

"Hmm. Is that another promise?"

Ryan laughed softly and then groaned when it set off another round of clenching contractions along the walls of her pussy, doing a delicious little massage up the sensitive length of his cock. "Yeah, baby. That's another promise."

And one he intended to keep.

Chapter Ten

Ryan was starting to doze, a warm, heavy feeling of contentment like he'd never experienced flowing through him as Shea snuggled in his arms. He'd never felt after sex, the way he did with her. Hell, it'd always felt good, yeah, but it'd never left him so ridiculously happy—and it'd sure as hell never felt this good.

They'd finally made it off the table and back to her bed, and now one of her hands rested on his chest, skimming through the curly hair in an oddly arousing caress that he felt straight down to his toes. He should've been dead to the world already, but when her thumb flicked over his right nipple, his breath sharpened with the resulting jolt of sensation and his cock twitched in ready agreement.

Her touch was curious, tender—a way he'd never been touched before—and his body didn't think twice about responding.

Hell, he thought with a wry groan, *this isn't natural.*

It felt like they'd been screwing for days, and she was so damn tight his cock was actually sore. Of course, it was sore in a good way.

A really, really good way.

Shea smoothed her hand down Ryan's muscle-sculpted stomach, marveling at the hard beauty of his body, the feel of his firm skin beneath her palm. Unable to resist the temptation, wanting so badly to study him as closely as he'd studied her, she raised up on one arm beside him. Then she took a deep, excitement-filled breath and trailed her hand straight down to his groin.

Hah! How was that for bold and daring?

His hair there was a beautiful golden brown, and she couldn't resist running her fingers through it, just as she'd done on his chest. Ryan's powerful body shifted beneath her touch, restless with anticipation, his muscles bunching and relaxing with the steady increase in his breathing.

He wanted it — this — and knowing that made her want it even more.

She knew his dark blue gaze burned on her with curious intensity, but wasn't ready to raise her eyes, not wanting to lose her nerve or be sucked under by the potent force of his will.

She trailed her fingers along his impressive length, and then dipped into the wet slit in the tip, licking her lips as she thought about how sweet it was going to be when she rooted her tongue into that glistening little hole. She wanted his taste in her mouth — wanted to feel the power of that magnificent cock fucking her face, spurting down her throat. Funny, 'cause the idea of giving head had never really played a part in her fantasies before now. It'd always been something she'd imagined she'd do for her partner, instead of for herself.

But suddenly she couldn't think of anything in the world sexier than having his cock between her lips, tasting those pearly drops of pre-cum on her tongue.

As if he knew what she was thinking, Ryan groaned her name in a warning growl that she smilingly ignored. Twisting her curls over one shoulder, she smoothed her soft palm over the long, still growing length of his cock, explored the heavy sacs beneath, then leaned down and closed her lips around the glistening head.

Ryan made a hoarse, harsh sound of male satisfaction, gritting his teeth hard to keep from coming in her face. He'd already been sporting a hopeful hard-on, but the sweet touch of her lips sent his blood heaving, surging— his cock rising tall and proud, begging for attention as if he hadn't just experienced God knew how many mind-blowing orgasms in the past twenty-four hours. Hell, she'd turned him into a fucking sex maniac. He grew even more, loving the way her lips were stretched wide around his width, her sweet mouth barely able to take him in.

Shea licked him experimentally, kind of surprised to discover how much she enjoyed his musky male scent and taste. Seeking more of it, she rooted her tongue into the slit she found on the large, blunt head, and Ryan jolted so hard in reaction he nearly dumped her to the floor. Then his hands found her hair, twisting into the curly mass of it, and Shea gave an inward smile of womanly delight when he held her in place, urging her to take more of him.

"Hell, Shea, you're killing me, baby. Take more. Oh, shit, please—just like that."

She opened her jaws as wide as they'd go and worked to draw him into her mouth, but his monstrous size and her relative inexperience made the action frustratingly difficult. She licked him instead, swirling her tongue greedily around the now juicy tip, and was rewarded by a long, ragged moan.

Keeping her lips against him, she teased him with the delicate scrape of her teeth, the hungry lapping of her tongue. "You taste so good."

Another masculine grunt floated down to her, and her woman's pride shook her fists in the air, loving the control she wielded over his pleasure.

"I can't believe all of this fits inside of me, making me scream, feeling so good. I love it, the way you make me feel, Ry. It's like there's something wild and primitive that's been unleashed that I never knew was there."

Ryan tried to make some glib, teasing comment in return. Anything to lighten the alarming web of emotion weaving around him, but all that would emerge from his panting mouth was another ragged groan. Damn, she was fucking killing him, and any second now he was going to lose it.

He struggled harder for control, knowing he was on the edge of something profound—someplace he'd never been before—and it scared the hell out of him.

He knew he wanted Shea. Aw hell—he even wanted her to fall in love with him.

Wanted it a lot.

As in more than anything.

But there was no way in hell he was going to let her turn him into some kind of pathetic, lovesick ass. He had to remember that, but it wasn't easy when she was giving him the sweetest head he'd ever had. His muscles tightened, shuddering in need, and his dick felt like it was about to turn itself inside out at the soft, wet touch of her lips and tongue. "*Ah...fuck!*"

Her touch was growing bolder, her hand tightening around him as much as it could. He was so thick, she couldn't even fully enclose him with her fingers, and so long that the blunt, heart-shaped head reached up high onto his muscled stomach.

"It's true," Shea whispered, her voice a seductive purr. "I mean—well, you're huge." Her hand moved down to gently cradle his balls again, her touch exquisitely curious, as if she'd never really taken the time to explore a man before him. "Enormous, actually."

A harsh sound—part laugh, part growl—burst from his throat. "Damn, you're trying to kill me, aren't you? And I'm perfectly normal, you crazy little innocent. I just know how to use what I've got."

And please God, let her believe it. In some irrational part of his sex-fried brain, Ryan was almost terrified she'd find out just how big he really was and decide to find a man easier to take. *Over my dead body*, he vowed with savage resolve, knowing he could easily dismember anyone who ever tried to take her away from him. Look what had almost happened with Spalding. If Shea and Derek hadn't gotten in his way, he'd have torn the bastard limb from limb without a second thought.

She moved, crouching on her hands and knees between his bent legs, staring at his cock as if it were the eighth wonder of the world. Then she lowered her head again and licked from his sacs all the way up the long length, until she was pulling him in again, trying to draw him deeper. "Damn it," she moaned, unable to take as much as she wanted. "You're too big for this."

Ryan gave a strained laugh at her put-out tone, thinking it was just about the sexiest thing in the world, knowing Shea wanted to give him head. He fisted one hand in her curls, pulling her mouth back where he wanted it, and touched the rim with the fingers of his other hand, stroking her lips while she tried again. She looked up at him, swallowing over five thick inches of cock, her mouth stretched full with barely half of him, and he knew he'd never wanted a woman the way he wanted her. Hell, it was like she'd been made just for him to tongue and fuck and love.

"More," he grunted through his clenched teeth.

Her brows knitted and she glared up at him, her look clearly saying, *Hey, big boy, I'm trying here.*

His hand fisted tighter, holding her head still as he pushed deeper, shocking those smoky eyes of hers wide. "I said more, Shea. Relax your throat...that's it...just suck it down. Damn, you deep-throat like a fucking pro, honey. You sure you've never done this before?"

The second the words were out of his mouth, Ryan recognized them as a big fucking mistake. He knew he sounded like a jackass, but then this newfound, bizarre sense of possessiveness roared through him, rearing its ugly head, pushing him, and he heard himself say, "You suck it better than any other woman I've ever known." Her eyes were telling him to go to hell while she tried to pull back, but he just held her tighter, keeping her gagged with his cock.

"You put your all into it, baby, like you really enjoy having this pretty little mouth stuffed full of dick. You like to swallow it too, don't you? I wonder how many guys you've teased like this, thinking they were gonna get a chance at that sweet little cunt of yours, only to cut 'em cold in the end? Because God knows just having you look at me makes me want to come all over you. You really are a little cock-tease, aren't you, Shea?"

Her teeth closed down the barest bit, adding a bit of pain with the pleasure, but he didn't think she'd actually bite him. No, she liked fucking him too much to take a chance on injuring him, no matter how deadly the look in her eyes. Still, Ry wasn't taking any chances with his dick, and slowly released his grip on her head, letting her slip off of him. He watched her under lowered brows as she sat back on her heels, wiping the back of her hand across her wet mouth.

"You're being a pig and an asshole, you know that?"

"Yeah," he muttered, gripping her wrist when she went to move away. "So I've been told before. But you suck my cock like you don't really give a shit, sweetheart, so as long as I let you have it. You sure you haven't been going down on guys to get more experience before moving on to me, because you seem to know a hell of a lot more about giving head than you do about fucking!"

Shea stiffened at his deliberately cruel words, wondering why he was still trying to hurt her. She looked away and struggled to draw her hand away from his. "Just because I've never done it before doesn't mean I can't like it," she replied coolly. "So I like the taste of your cock. So what? It doesn't mean I go around blowing every guy I meet."

He didn't care for the ice princess tone of her voice. "Yeah, well, it doesn't mean you haven't done your fair share of sucking guys off, either."

"I've read about it, you jerk!" she growled with a small shrug, still trying to pull away from him. "Jesus, I told you—just because I don't have your sordid sexual history doesn't mean I'm an idiot. I read books and go to movies, Ry, just like everybody else. I may have been pretty inexperienced, but that doesn't mean I'm deaf and blind too!"

Then, with surprising strength, she managed to wrench her hand free and roll out of the bed in one fluid motion despite the various aches in her sex-ravaged body. She stared down at his sprawled form with an expression that fell somewhere between hurt and furious.

"Besides, you're one to talk, McCall. From what I've seen and heard, you go to bed with anything that moves, so long as it has a pulse. You're probably the biggest whore I know, and yet you're ready to yell at me because you think I like giving head. And the fact that I haven't gone down on anyone but you isn't even the issue. The issue's that you're insulting and hypocritical and—"

Before she was able to take two steps, Ryan had her pinned beneath him. She stared up at him in shock; her body trapped in place by the solid press of male bone and muscle, his cock a hard, demanding weight against her thigh.

"Damn it, I'm sorry. I don't know what it is, but you make me crazy. I didn't mean to say those things. I was just—shit, I was jealous."

"You? Right," she scoffed, clearly not believing a word of it. "You may be an asshole, but I don't think you have a jealous bone in your body. You probably can't wait for me to find some other guy to fuck, can you? I bet the pressure of being one of the few men I've screwed is already wearing you thin, huh, Ry?"

"That just goes to show how much you know about men, sugar, because I'd kill anyone who so much as laid a fucking finger on you. If that's not jealousy, then I don't know what the hell is. All I know is that I can't stand the thought of you with another man, touching him the way you've touched me. And the thought of any man but me touching you or eating you or fucking you makes me crazy," he snarled in a strange tone, like he couldn't believe he was actually revealing such a thing to her.

"Ryan," she breathed softly, trying to sort through what he'd said—revealed. She smoothed her palms down the sleekly muscled line of his back, not sure whether she wanted to smack him or kiss him. "Don't you get it yet? I don't want anyone but you."

"Ah, that's good, then," he replied with a slow, sexy smile, catching the wisps of curls at her temples and gently tucking them behind her ears, ruefully aware that his fingers were shaking. "Because you're mine now, Shea. Whether you like it or not. *Mine*. And I don't share, sweetheart. Just ask my Mom. I used to beat the crap outta any kid who tried to play with my toys."

"Hmm, I don't know if you've, ah, noticed—but I'm not a toy, Agent McCall."

"Maybe not," he drawled with another devastating smile, the look of heat in his dark blue eyes making her burn. He pushed her slender, silky thighs wide and entered her for the fourth time that day, determined to show her just how much. "But I do love playing with you."

He knew she must be sore. God knew his dick felt raw from all the physical excess. Not that he wasn't used to going all night long, but Shea's cunt was so damn tight it made one screw feel like ten. She was swollen and small and his entry still wasn't any easier, but she didn't complain. She just held his eyes, her look revealing how much she loved the way he ruthlessly worked himself in. The insistent push and penetration made her pant and moan, while he trembled at the feel of her. She felt so perfect, so right, so *his*.

When she had taken every inch, he stopped and stared down at her as if she were the most precious thing in the entire world to him. And he made her feel precious. Made her feel beautiful and sexy and like a woman. She rubbed her palms down his smooth back again, loving the feel of his warm skin, the life and energy and strength that was so Ryan. Then she gripped the hard-muscled curve of his buttocks and pulled him even deeper inside.

His eyes blazed, his nostrils flared, and his cock leapt up into her. "Damn it, Shea. You're unmanning me, babe."

Her newfound power felt wonderful, and she couldn't resist the sexy smile that broke across her face. Trying a technique she'd once read about in Cosmo, she tightened her inner muscles and squeezed the thick, solid length of his cock where it was packing her so full, filling her up.

Ryan gasped, grunted, then swore foully. Twisting his fingers into her hair, he held her head in place while he groaned against her lips. "Jesus, do it again."

She did, marveling at the stark look of pleasure washing over his fierce features.

"Fuck," he growled in a savage voice, pulling out of her. "I was going to be gentle this time, but you drive me over the edge, woman."

Before she understood his intent, Ryan had her pushed to her stomach and positioned on her knees, with her legs still spread wide and her face buried in the wrecked bedding. She twisted to look at him over her shoulder and could hear the shy uncertainty in her own voice as she gasped, "Ryan, what—"

"Trust me." And with those two words, she felt like the helpless little lamb being reeled in by the big, bad, hungry wolf.

Ryan's hot palms grasped her bottom, and then moved lower, opening the lips of her cunt with his thumbs until she knew he could see all of her. His deep voice was hard bitten with authority, leaving no room for argument. "Arch your back and lift this rosy little ass up in the air for me."

Shea trembled under his touch as his hands molded over her, branding her with beauty and possession. Her weeping pussy grew hotter, wetter, until she was dripping like warm honey down the insides of her thighs, sweet and syrupy.

Ryan's fingers moved over her, lightly pinching her clit and smearing her moisture over sensitive tissues, torturing them both. "You really do have the most gorgeous little cunt I've ever seen, Shea. It's like something from a fucking fantasy, so pink and ripe and always begging to be tongue-fucked. I could eat out this juicy slit for the rest of my life and still never get enough of it."

She moaned at his words, horrifyingly aroused—or was it arousingly horrified? Before she could decide, she was screaming at the blissful feel of his tongue lapping at her, plunging within, collecting her sweet, copious juice and his fluids mixed with her own.

He showed her with the greedy demands of his lips and tongue and teeth how much he loved going down on her, eating her out, making it obvious that he took as much pleasure from the intimately carnal act as she did. Seeking a lifeline, Shea's hands dug into the sheets, clawing at white cotton for leverage in a world that was quickly spinning out of control.

Brilliant bursts of color began to dance behind her closed lids as he repeatedly took her to the maddening brink of climax without letting her fly over the edge. She gasped and moaned, her meaning understood even if the breathy pleas were unclear. Then, when she simply couldn't take it anymore, she heard herself shouting words she'd never in all her life thought she'd have the daring to say. "Fuck me, Ry! Oh, God...please! Get in me!" she screamed. "Get your cock in me!"

"Hold on," Ryan growled, fitting the dripping head of his cock to the streaming mouth of her greedy cunt. "For fuck's sake, just hold on!" The knot in his dick doubled— tripled, on the verge of bursting apart as he prepared to give her exactly what she wanted and fuck her raw. He thrust hard and deep, moving as if he intended to shove himself right through her, flesh through flesh, straight out the other side. Her hot little pussy clenched around him, squeezing like a fucking vise, daring him to take everything he wanted—everything she demanded.

Shit, a man couldn't get any luckier than having his woman demand he fuck her brains out. All the physical aches and pains of the weekend disappeared. They faded away on waves of pure sensation. He was glowing, pure fire pumping through his veins as he dug his fingers into her silky hips and let his hammering cock teach her insatiable cunt exactly who it belonged to—who would always own it.

No more ice man. No more fucking cold.

Ryan set his teeth in her shoulder, pulled out, and rammed in again, claiming her with his body the way he longed to claim her with his heart. She was screaming, crying, clawing at the covers, but they were all demands for more. She was dripping in sex juice, creamy and wet, soaking them both.

"You asked for this!" he growled, pumping her so full she was amazed she didn't rip open.

"I know," she groaned, her voice choppy and raw. "And I love it. Give me more, Ry. Give me more of it."

He took her at her word and dipped his fingers between their bodies, coating them in slippery juices, and then rubbing them into the tight little bud of her ass.

She jolted beneath him, shocked, unsure, but then he had her clit beneath the thumb of his other hand, digging it in, grinding against her, and those other two wicked fingers were pushing deep into her. They were pressing some kind of switch inside of her that set the muscles in her pussy clenching around him like a clamp, and she couldn't concentrate on anything except how good they felt and how full she was of Ryan.

"No tongue this time, angel. This time, you get the full treatment."

The long digits dug deeper, spearing into her, choking her with outrageous pleasure as his wicked tongue licked a hungry line along the column of her throat. "I'll shove my tongue up this tight little bud again, over and over, until you're dripping and begging to have it filled, but not right now. Right now I need it fast. I'm going to fuck it with my fingers, working it open until you're ready, and then I'm going to cram this sweet little ass so full of cock, you're gonna feel it pushing at the back of your throat." She trembled beneath him, and he grunted, "Does that scare you, Shea?"

"N-no," she moaned, unable to disguise the quiver of hunger in her husky voice. "You don't scare me."

"Good," he grunted, feeling his cock swell to bursting, wondering if the damn thing would explode, "because there's no way in hell I could keep it from happening. Not tonight. Not with you."

He pressed down with the thick fingers buried in her ass, working them in all the way, growling when he felt the pressure of those two big digits digging into his dick. "Fuck," he shouted, screwing his eyes shut, struggling to keep from coming too soon. He wanted this to last as long as it could, and if the sexy little cries spilling out of Shea's mouth were any indication, so did she. She wriggled her hips, adding to the sensation around his cock, and he sobbed out something that sounded like, "That's so fucking good."

Then he began to move again. His deliciously bruising, brutal thrusts pounded her cunt with pleasure, powerful and unrestrained, moving them up the bed until she had to brace herself against the headboard because his own hands were too busy to do it for her.

"You like that?" he grunted, withdrawing and plunging his fingers in tandem with his pounding, burgeoning shaft. "You like having this tight little ass finger-fucked, don't you, baby?"

"Yes," she sobbed, pumping her hips harder, working against him, driving him deeper. "Yes!"

"You ready for more?"

"All of it," she sobbed, her body wrenching, twisting atop the sheets in its desperation for completion. "*Anything.*"

He shuddered against her back, his slick skin slipping against hers in a delicious friction of muscle and flesh. One second he was drilling into her, parting the tight channel of her pussy thrust after thrust, and in the next he was pulling free of the wet, suctioning grasp.

Shea tried not to stiffen up, knowing what was coming next, ready for it—even hungry for it, but still nervous. Ryan's cock was massive, and though his thick fingers felt good as they slipped free from her backside, she still wasn't completely certain she could take something as large as his full-sized erection. She took a deep, panting breath, trying to relax her muscles, only to let out an embarrassing shriek of alarm at the first press of the wet head against the tight rosebud.

"Just breathe with me," he murmured, his voice like rough silk, stroking over her skin, and she fell under the spell of raw sensuality he was weaving around them. The air and their heated bodies smelled sweetly erotic, the melody of their moans filling the silence of the night, and she succumbed—willingly.

One large palm pressed up against the center of her chest, between her swaying breasts, moving with the rhythm of her lungs. "Breathe with me," he repeated, his chest expanding against her back as his own lungs filled with air, and as they exhaled in unison, the broad head of his cock pressed into her in a delicious stretch that had heat leaping to an inferno in her veins, pumping through her body in a fevered rush of ecstasy and sensation.

"Oh my God," she groaned, breathing with him, and each time they exhaled he pushed deeper, working the thick intrusion of his cock into the tight recess until it was buried halfway up inside of her. Her burning muscles clamped down on it so hard, they both gritted their teeth from the tender, painful pleasure—and then the pace changed, his control slipping away as he began to move in a helpless, relentless rhythm.

His hips pulled back, and then he sank in another two inches, the pleasure exploding through her body, sharp and satisfying.

"I'm sorry—I can't hold back," he groaned, his hips picking up speed, pushing her harder with each greedy thrust. She struggled to answer, but could only pant louder. And then all she could do was cry out in need as his hand hooked around the front of her mound again, two fingers pinching her swollen clit, working it into a frenzy of pumping need.

Her hands clawed into the bedding, her back arched, and suddenly she was helping him, pushing back against his burrowing cock until she'd taken him to the root, stuffed full of his throbbing flesh.

"Fuck...you'll kill me," he growled, his lust-filled voice full of wonder as he slowly withdrew, pressed back in, withdrew, then pressed harder, until they were once again moving in a vicious, violent need for every ounce of pleasure and sensation they could wring from the passionate encounter. An intensely erotic experience they both knew they'd want...*need*...again and again.

The tighter she gripped him, the harder he rode and stroked her, until they were groaning and shouting and grinding together in another volcanic, earth-shattering, ground-shifting release. Ryan shot up into her in a powerful blast of cum that had her shaking beneath him, her muscles contracting tighter and tighter as his wicked fingers propelled her into an orgasm so strong, she thought she must have passed out.

Time was lost, forgotten, and when she came back to reality, he was falling to his side as he carried her down with him in the tight circle of his arms, crushing her back to his chest—his cock still nestled up tight within her body, content in its place, as if it belonged there. They were sticky and wet with cum, sealed together from their fluids in a poignant, emotional melding of bodies that neither wanted to end.

Neither spoke, but the idea of words seemed such a harsh intrusion into so meaningful a silence. They drifted, together, lost in the moment—and a little in awe of it.

Later, after some awkward maneuvering and a quick run through the shower, Shea lay warm and soft in his arms again, sleeping against his chest in utter exhaustion, while Ryan struggled to regain some sort of grip on reality. Damn, he was so far out there, flying on the biggest high of his life, but terrified he was going to make a complete jackass of himself. This couldn't be good, because it was too fucking good.

The woman in his arms had become his entire friggin' existence—completely blindsiding him.

She sighed against his chest, snuggled closer against him, and he wanted to take her all over again. No, not good at all. He'd been too damn rough with her, which was putting it lightly considering the way he'd nailed her sweet little ass, and she *did* need some downtime, even if his insatiable prick didn't give a fuck. Come to think of it, her precious little cunt probably wouldn't protest another go either, greedy little thing that it was, but he was going to be gallant, even if it killed him.

Trying not to think about it, he sifted his fingers through the soft strands of her silky curls, loving the way they felt. Loving the warm press of her body against his, the moist heat of her sex-swollen cunt against his hip, her soft thigh draped over his aching cock. Jesus, he was in love with her. He knew it, felt it, but he couldn't accept it. Not yet. No way in hell.

He knew he wanted Shea, but there was no sense rushing this—this thing between them. Especially when she had this irrational, terrifying, utterly consuming hold on him. He needed time to work it out, time to learn how to handle it without making an utter ass of himself. They could take their time. Take it easy. Work up to living together, and in the meantime, he'd have her close.

Hell, she was right next door. He'd be able to see her every day, sleep beside her every night. They could even take turns whose apartment they stayed at. He'd make it clear their relationship would remain exclusive, and eventually they'd take those next steps.

Eventually.

Ryan's arms held her closer, crushing her to him as he tried to ignore the disturbing feeling that it wasn't going to be enough, that he needed those other steps now. It had to be, damn it, because he just wasn't ready to throw his heart out on the line. He could only hope Shea felt the same—or hell, that she felt anything at all.

After what seemed like hours of trying to work this thing out in his mind, Ryan finally felt the need for sleep. Taking care not to hurt her, he gave in to the urge and gently pushed his cock back up inside of her, needing to feel it wrapped up warmly in her body where it belonged. He pressed a gentle kiss to her temple and her swollen mouth, luxuriating in the ecstasy of having her close, of being buried deep inside her with her scent surrounding him. Then he fell into a deep sleep with his body touching hers, inside and out, skin sealed to skin, heart against heart.

Chapter Eleven

She had had him for a week.

The best damn week of her life.

But it wasn't enough.

Not nearly enough. Oh, she'd experienced enough mind-shattering physical sensation to blow every brain cell she had, but her heart wanted more.

Her heart wanted it all.

It wanted the throbbing pulse of pleasure that he forced down her nerve endings until she was screaming and writhing in blood-pounding ecstasy, his wickedly talented cock teaching her things she'd never even known about herself. The limitless lust and need and ravenous, insatiable, demanding hunger he could pound through her system, making her beg and plead for the warm, sweet, clenching gush of orgasm until her throat ached. Making her plead until they were a grinding, pounding union of skin, sweat, and eager mouths and hands that couldn't get enough of each other—not to mention cock and cunt that seemed to never want to separate.

It was a passionate, sexual heaven. A physically decadent paradise. A pure, blissful perfection of everything she had known she would find in Ryan McCall's arms. He gave her everything—all that he was—except for that one part she wanted more than anything.

His damn stubborn heart.

Throughout the long week, he'd called her on her cell during her breaks between classes, just to talk with her. Sometimes their conversations were playful, teasing, and yet others were just a sweet, simple sharing of their days. They'd laugh about the latest staff room rumor and he'd bitch about the snag in his latest case. It was surprising how she looked forward to those moments almost as much as the physical ones—just learning about his life and day-to-day routine. He was so funny and sexy and exciting to be around—and everything she'd felt for him leading up to last Friday night had only intensified over the course of the last seven days.

And then yesterday, he'd nearly made her come by the sound of his voice alone, in the middle of the university's cafeteria, as he described in explicit, delicious detail how they were going to sixty-nine when they got home that night. Despite all they'd done—all she'd experienced at his hands—that was still one sweet spot that they'd yet to explore. Something they'd kept just out of reach, letting the slow, sweet burn of anticipation build. Ryan's deep voice, so rough and suggestive, had set her on edge, and his promised words had kept her in a state of constant arousal to the point where she'd felt she was going to either burst or melt into a pulsing puddle of need in her plastic chair.

It'd been one of their most erotic experiences yet, his husky point-by-point description of everything they would do. "I'm going to spread those pretty pussy lips, open you wide, and suck on your swollen clit until you're shaking and crying and that hot little cunt is soaked in your cream. And when you're jerking against my face, all wet and juicy, sucking my cock down your throat, sucking on it like you want to fucking swallow it, your hot little mouth packed full of it—then I'm going to give you my tongue and fuck that delicious hole until your juices are spilling all over me, sliding down my throat, fucking filling me up."

Damn, that man knew how to drive her wild. When her last class let out, she'd rushed home like a demon was on her ass and spent an hour soaking in a hot bath full of vanilla scented bubbles, careful to avoid her pulsing, aching clit—wanting to stretch the anticipation out for all it was worth.

And when he'd walked through her door, his hands already going to the buttons of his fly, fingers ripping them loose as fast as they'd go, his sinful blue eyes eating her alive, she'd flooded with cream, the telling juices trickling down her thighs. He'd growled a feral sound of hunger when he'd reached her, her flimsy robe gone within the span of a breath, and then they'd been rolling across her late great aunt's Oriental carpet, lips and tongues and limbs tangling in a carnal demand of flesh and lust. She couldn't even recall how they'd made it from standing to lying, her senses too absorbed with hunger for the taste and scent of his hard, warm body as skin and muscle shifted in their urgent movements against one another.

His mouth had been everywhere, licking and kissing as if he were starved for every inch of her, every delicate nuance of her body. Ravenous for everything that made her so different from every other woman he'd ever known. The sensitive skin behind her ears. The back of her neck and her pierced little navel. The insides of her elbows. The hollows of her hipbones.

When they finally shifted, mouths to throbbing cock and sweet, slippery cunt, Shea had thought she would die from the rush of pure, erotic awareness.

And all the while, Ryan had rasped hot, detailed, sexy commands against the sensitive flesh of her pussy, telling her what to do, teaching her how to draw it out until they were both trembling with desperation, their bodies slick with need. And when he couldn't take it anymore, when she'd driven him beyond his limit, he'd growled out his demands, firing her with the desire to blow his mind.

Oh, shit…more, baby.

Deeper.

All the way down — suck it in.

Fucking suck it deep.

More…more…more.

And she'd moaned with savage satisfaction when she finally pushed him over the edge and they flooded into one another, coming with such force they'd nearly shouted themselves hoarse.

Then the wicked man had taken her pleasure-sated body into his arms, made her heart flutter at the sweet, soft touch of his warm lips against her own, carried her into her bedroom, and promptly handcuffed her to her headboard!

At first she'd been stunned, giggling at his playfulness as he stretched out above her, whispering devilish sentiments in her ear. Then he'd made her come so many times with his clever fingers and tongue that she was crying and cursing, begging for the feel of his cock inside of her. And when he'd finally let her have it—parting the tight muscles of her pussy with his thick root—she'd come so hard she'd passed out, only to awaken to him giving her those soft, sweet kisses again, whispering silly little words about how beautiful she was…how delicious.

How much he always wanted her.

How he only wanted her more every damn time he had her.

But it hadn't gone beyond that. She hadn't even set foot in his apartment, because he'd yet to invite her there. Every evening Ryan came to her straight from work, they'd eat dinner together, spend the night screwing each other's brains out, and in the morning he would run home to change before heading back to work.

And now it was Friday again, damn it, and Shea wanted to know just what in the hell was going on. This was what she wanted—and so much less. She wanted it all, damn it! Wanted everything! But for all she knew, he'd be heading back to Red's tonight. And if not tonight—then when? And what was she willing to do about it when he did?

He'd said all he wanted was to fuck her, and by God, he had. Oh, had he ever. As she dragged her tired body through her apartment, slipping off her shoes, tossing her backpack into the corner of her bedroom, every carnal act they'd done together flashed through her mind in a torrent of vividly detailed images.

Ryan with his mouth at her breasts, sucking at her nipples as if he meant to devour them.

Ryan with his head buried between her thighs, probing deeply with his tongue while his thumbs held her wide open for him, unable to get enough of her taste.

Ryan propped up on his arms above her while they both watched the hard, savage thrust of his body into hers.

Everything they'd done had been about mind-blowing physical pleasure—and yet, it'd felt like more than just incredible sex, as if he'd been trying to tell her something with his body that he either couldn't or wouldn't say with words.

It made her so damn angry and frustrated—his refusal to open up. She'd tried to tell him how she felt that first night, but he hadn't wanted to hear it, and he wasn't going to say it himself. She had to find a way to reach him—had to get past that stubborn-ass armor of his or she was going to lose him before she ever even had him.

And she was no quitter.

That was another one of those wonderful things Ryan did for her. When she was with him, she felt more confident—more certain of herself—like she could take on the world, if that's what she wanted.

It was odd, considering he was such a big, beautiful, dominating man, but he didn't treat her like a weak doormat to walk on and use. He treated her like a sassy, sexy woman and she felt more powerful for it. She'd been more outrageous and daring and full of life in the past week than in the entire last twenty-seven years, and she knew it was because of him. Not that it was his doing, exactly, but more like—like his influence on her. Being near him, a part of him, was good for her. She was stronger for it, a better person for it.

So then why was she moping around with her tail between her legs, waiting for him to make his move?

How much more pathetic could she get?

Screw this, she thought with a disgusted growl. She was *not* going to play the pathetic weakling here and let him get away that easily. No, she was going to dig in, show him what she was made of, and rock his world until he didn't know whether he was coming or going. She just had to remember to keep her emotions out of it, at least until the time was right and he was ready to hear what she had to say.

A part of her deep inside knew that he might never be ready, but she was just going to have to be woman enough to stand up and take it.

And, of course, change his mind.

With that thought clutched to her chest like a talisman, Shea strolled into her bathroom for a quick shower, ready to put her final plan into motion.

Chapter Twelve

He'd forgotten his effing umbrella. It figured, after the afternoon he'd had drudging through old case files and wrapping up paperwork, that the sky would decide to unload on him now. And shit, he was in too much of a hurry to get home to Shea to worry about getting soaked in the downpour.

He'd just stepped out into the biting, gray rain when his cell began buzzing against his hip bone. Jogging over to his truck, he climbed up into the humid interior of the cab and cranked the engine to get the windows defrosted, cursing the tiny silver phone for being so damn small. How the hell was he supposed to talk into something no bigger than a freaking business card?

Or maybe his hands were just too damn big.

"McCall," he muttered into the insubstantial mouthpiece, grinding his jaw as images of his "big" hands moving over Shea's soft skin flooded through his memory, singeing his already sensory jammed system. She'd been burned into his consciousness—her taste, her smell, the feel of her naked flesh against his own—all of it was right there, pounding in his temples, pumping to the rapid beat of his heart.

He'd had a lot to think about today, starting with the crack of the morning phone call from Hannah. When his cell had begun vibrating on the bedside table, he'd carefully disengaged his cock from Shea's warm pussy, loving the way they had often slept that way throughout the week, and walked into her living room to take the call.

He'd known who it would be without even looking at the caller id, wondering if Hannah was gonna make it a habit of keeping tabs on his and Shea's sex life from now on. Her grandmother had taken a turn for the worse, and so she'd yet to make it back from Tennessee.

"Still there, huh? Just tell me I'm not going to have to come home and go kung-fu on your ass." Hannah's voice had been loud and clear, making Ryan wince from the jolt to his sleep-dazed system. Shit, the damn woman had sounded like she'd already had a gallon of caffeine, and he'd been working on a real bitch of a sex hangover.

The thought of it brought a smile to his face now — just as it had that morning. They'd fucked all week long, too many times to count, and his body was feeling deliciously used in all the right places. But last night — Jesus, last night had nearly killed him.

He'd run a hand through his hair, still smiling when he'd said, "Naw, no butchering will be necessary. And since when did you become such a pit bull?"

"Since my oldest best friend started sleeping with my newest best friend and she's — " Hannah's voice had trailed uncomfortably off into silence.

"She's what?" Ryan had asked distractedly, trying to snag a look at Shea's kitchen clock, anxious to get over to the court house and file his latest report on Spalding so it wouldn't take up too much of his day. He and Derek had an important meeting this morning with the D.A.'s office about the case, and the sooner Spalding's ass got convicted and put behind bars for a good long while, the better.

And he'd figured the sooner he got back home, the more time he'd have to spend with Shea tonight. Then tomorrow. Then the day after that—and the rest of his life.

Funny, but that thought no longer made him clench up with fear the way it had a week ago.

Hannah had been silent for a moment, then taken a deep breath and muttered, "Never mind. You're going to have to figure this one out on your own, Ry."

That conversation had played through his mind all damn day, and she'd apparently called back to get out whatever it was she'd wanted to say, because the first words out of her mouth this time were, "Okay, have you told her how you feel yet?"

"Ah...no," he muttered, hating that he was feeling kinda tongue-tied about the subject, and wondering just what in the hell Hannah was getting at.

There was a pause—one in which his heart began beating like a friggin' bass drum—and then she said in a rush, as if she had to force the words out quickly, "Shea's probably going to kill me for this, but if I don't help you out here, you're going to completely screw this up. So...what I'm trying to say is...well, I think you should know she's in love with you. It's not just lust for her, Ry. She's madly, totally *in love* with you—the head over heels, happily ever after kind. So don't even think about breaking her heart or hurting her, because if you do, I promise I'll make you sorry."

Ryan blinked in surprise, his heart one shockingly hard, resounding beat in his chest. "Huh?" he muttered stupidly, his blown brainwaves unable to come up with anything more intelligent or insightful to say. Finally, he managed to grunt, "Well, if that's true, she sure as hell hasn't mentioned it to me."

"Gee, I wonder why? She already believes you're going to break her heart when you're through with her. And she isn't an idiot. She's smart and beautiful and full of life. She'll protect herself, and that means she'll keep her feelings to herself, no matter how much of a temptation you might be."

"And how the hell would you know?"

There was silence, and then, in a low voice, Hannah said, "I know it's hard for you to remember at times, Ry, but I am a woman. I may not believe in fairy tales anymore, but I know when I see true love. I know when I see something that's real. And this woman is my best friend, so I'd like to think I've got a good understanding of her."

For the first time in their entire friendship, Ryan heard a real thread of fury in Hannah's husky voice. "I'd really been holding out hope that you wouldn't let her get away, but if all you're looking for is a good fuck, then stay the hell away from her. She doesn't deserve to be used and tossed aside. She's something special. She deserves someone who can give her more."

"And if that person's me?" he grunted, suddenly no longer caring if he made a fool out of himself.

More silence, and then a soft, almost inaudible sigh. "Jesus, you're serious, aren't you? She's really gotten to you, hasn't she? I mean—you actually want her for more than just some raunchy time between the sheets, don't you?"

Ryan snorted. "Don't get me wrong, Hannah. I want the raunchy sex, no two ways about it. I want to nail her more than I've ever wanted anything—*anything* in my entire life." His eyes closed as he laid his head back on the headrest and took a slow, deep breath. "But it's more than that. I want *her*," he muttered, unable to stop the flow of words spilling out of his mouth. "I want to live with her and sleep with her and take care of her. I want to own her and I want everyone to know it, and I want her to own me. I want to be responsible for her, Hannah. I want it all. I want everything."

Even though she couldn't see him, he felt his face go hot, uncomfortable and unsure, but refused to be embarrassed about revealing so much of himself. God knew she'd unloaded her female troubles on him enough times over the years. Hell, it was only fair that he get a turn.

Hannah laughed—a soft, happy sound—and he knew that it was for him, that she was honestly happy for him, which made him a pretty lucky bastard to have such an incredible friend in his life. Too bad he had to be a miserable, broken-hearted bastard as well—if it turned out that Shea didn't feel the same way about him. "You've actually done it, honey. You've finally let that bitch Kelly stop ruining your life and fallen in love."

"Yeah, well," he grumbled. "I wouldn't go celebrating just yet. She hasn't admitted jack shit about how she feels to me, remember? Maybe you're wrong."

"Stop being such a chicken shit and go tell her how you feel, you big oaf. That woman's loved you since the moment she first set eyes on you."

And with that heart-jolting statement, the line disconnected. Ryan didn't know how long he sat there trembling with the biggest, goofiest grin splitting his face, feeling like an idiot but too happy to give a damn. Shea loved him? No, wait—Hannah had said Shea was *madly in love with him*!!!

Holy shit!

But what if she was wrong? His heart kept pounding like a son-of-a-bitch while he tried to sort it out. Had she meant the words that had almost tumbled from her mouth that first night, before he'd swallowed them with his kiss, cutting off whatever it was she would've said?

If she'd said she was in love with him, would it have been the truth?

And he knew it didn't have to do with finally letting go of the past. It was Shea. He could've spent the last fifteen years searching for love, and it wouldn't have mattered, because he wouldn't have had her.

And now he did.

Memories of the week crashed over him: her smiles, her laughter, their combustible physical chemistry—the mind-blowing hours they'd spent grinding against one another, sapping their bodies of strength as orgasm after orgasm had pounded through their systems.

But one of the sweetest of all—his favorite—was waking at odd hours to find her propped up beside him, her little book light set on dim while she read her school texts, obviously trying to get in her studying hours whenever she could, since he had staked such a monopoly on her evenings. He loved the way her sexy curls fell around her pretty face, her expression serious as she read about God only knew what. Her intelligence was so much a part of her, and he felt a strange, foreign pride in his chest at all she'd accomplished—all that she would. She was one hell of a woman, and he would lie there beside her, his body pressed to her side, arm wrapped possessively around her waist, pretending to sleep while watching her beneath his lashes, unable to take his eyes off of her.

Yeah, he was a lovesick ass, all right. The one thing he'd sworn he'd never, ever be.

And God help him, he no longer fucking cared.

All he cared about was going and getting his hands on his woman, and keeping them there forever.

Chapter Thirteen

By the time Ryan threw open his front door, he was nervous and shaking and damn near terrified. Finding Shea sitting on his sofa, reading a thick book on Alexander the Great, was nearly enough to do his knees in with relief.

He'd tried her cell phone five times on the way home, but she hadn't answered, and he'd already been to her apartment and nearly gone out of his mind when she was nowhere to be found.

And she'd been here all along, waiting for him.

God, he felt sick. Sick and scared and fucking furious that he'd waited so long to have this conversation.

He couldn't wait anymore.

He was going to explain a few things before screwing her senseless again. He'd start with the fact that he was in love with her, followed closely by the fact that he wanted to marry her. Considering they were two things he had sworn to never do again, he was nervous as hell about it.

No, he qualified with a hoarse groan, petrified was more like it, which had frustration surging through him all over again. Shit, she was tying him in knots without even trying. He felt like a flame springing to life in a room full of explosives. One wrong move and everything would be lost. And damn it, he'd already made enough wrong moves.

He'd screwed up, he knew it, by being such a jackass and not coming right out and telling her how he felt before now. He'd tried to play it cool and safe, just like some pitiful coward, hoping she'd open up and reveal her feelings first. He'd let fear and his dumb-ass pride control his actions, and it could've cost him big time.

If he waited any longer, he might lose her — and that was something he simply wasn't willing to accept.

A part of him, the part that had locked up his emotions for so damn long, felt like he was setting himself up for a huge emotional letdown here, but he couldn't backpedal fast enough to stop his heart from tumbling forward. Damn it, he couldn't be wrong this time. Not about this. Not about them. No way in hell.

He was willing to bet his fucking life on it — on her.

And she looked so beautiful sitting there that he just wanted to fall all over her. She looked like a gypsy...a poet...an ancient siren luring him to his doom all too easily. Damn, she didn't even have to try. One word, one look, and he'd be on his knees in front of her, drooling like a dog for a chance to push those silky thighs wide and feast on her sticky sweet little pussy until he was so full of her she was a part of him.

The air surrounding her was charmed with innocence, cloaking her in protection. Ryan gritted his teeth against the savage need to rip it down, shattering her resistance until she was wide open and vulnerable, reduced to the same gnawing need that ate at him from within. He wanted her wild and hungry and ready to fuck, and he wanted her now.

He wanted her forever.

But first he had to tell her how he felt, damn it — and he didn't know how the hell to do it.

Shea looked up to see him towering in the doorway. He hadn't bothered to knock, but then this *was* his home, and he'd obviously forgotten his umbrella, because his clothes dripped water onto the floor where he stood. His rain-soaked hair was plastered to his head, dripping water into his narrowed eyes. And his handsome face wore a thunderous look of equal parts outrage and what looked strangely like fear.

It was impossible to tell which storm was worse, the one raging outside the walls of his apartment or the one standing in the doorway. "Hello, Ryan," she said lamely, not a clue what to do. Damn, he was so beautiful it knocked the air right out of her and she drew a complete blank. Then her plan came back to her in a spark of intensity, and she closed the book, set it beside her, stood up and headed for his bedroom.

He followed her, feeling like an explosive ready to blow, the seconds to detonation ticking by faster and faster. "What are you doing here, Shea? Do you know how worried I was when I couldn't get you on your phone and you weren't at your place? How the hell did you even get in here?"

She shrugged casually, toeing off her sneakers and tossing them out of the way. "My phone's in my apartment, so I didn't hear it. As for how I got in here, I've got a key to Hannah's place, and Hannah's got a key to yours. Do you mind that I let myself in?" she asked huskily, her graceful fingers slowly unzipping her jeans, showing him she wore nothing underneath.

Ryan swallowed the growing lump of lust in his throat and felt his damn body clench in need, wanting to devour her whole. But he was trying to talk to her, damn it, not screw her! At least not yet. "What's this all about, Shea? You sound pissed."

"That's a stupid question, Ry. You said all you had to offer was sex, so I'm here to get it."

Well, shit. He didn't know what to make of her in this kind of mood, but his instincts were clueing in real quick to the fact that something here wasn't right. He needed to concentrate or he'd have her heels behind her ears, her pussy spread open and penetrated beneath him, before he knew what hit him.

He opened his mouth to ask what the hell she was talking about, but the sight of her tiny T-shirt being tossed over her head temporarily distracted him. By the time her jeans were clearing her ankles and her beautiful, naked little body was moving sinuously toward him, he'd completely forgotten they were even having a conversation. Well, at least he'd been trying to have one. Shea's only intent seemed to be getting into his pants, if the attention she was paying his fly was any indication.

Hell, it worked for him, and it definitely worked for his dick, which seemed to think it needed to set new records every time she was near. Her eyes were still dark, her cheeks flushed, the tasty flesh of her bottom lip pulled between her teeth as she started ripping the buttons of his fly open. His hands quickly lowered to join her own, his cock eager to get out and play. The last metal button slipped free, his dick poking through the open seam in his cotton boxers, huge and hard, ready to fuck, the tip already wet and ready. He reached for her, only to find himself falling backwards against his bed.

She'd pushed him—and the look in her eyes told him she planned on doing a hell of a lot more than that. Wondering if the expression on his face looked as stupid as it felt, Ry watched as she wrenched his jeans just over the swell of his hips, and then he couldn't see anything because his eyes rolled back in his head as she crawled over his legs and swallowed half his cock down her throat.

"Jesus Christ," he heard himself shout, his jaw grinding as her wet little tongue stroked him, her mouth moving up and down, cheeks hollowing out as she sucked him strong and sure, her hand coming up to gently cradle his balls, rolling the sacs in her palm. "Shea—oh, shit—I'm gonna come!"

It was a little embarrassing to be losing control so quickly, but Ryan didn't know how he was supposed to have any left when she sucked him as if she wanted to swallow him whole. His dick was pumping, warning him he didn't have long, but then her hand was squeezing tightly around the root of his cock, cutting off the flow, and she pulled off of him with one long, sensuous lick, making him want to beg for the finish. "Shea, what the fuck are you doing?"

And where the hell had she learned this little trick with her fingers to keep him from coming?

As if she read the question in his eyes, she licked her lips and said, "I read about it in a book. And just in case you were wondering, I'm not ready for you to come yet."

Then she crawled up him some more, planting her knees at his hips, and rubbed her warm, wet pussy across the tip of his cock, her hand still wrapped tight around its thick base. He made a rough, sharp choking sound, watching the way his head moved between the pussy-pink lips of her cunt, drenching him with cream, and she arched her back, tilting her hips forward to give him a better view.

"You like what you see, Ry?"

His eyes snapped to hers, hating the cold, calculating look he saw there. "Yeah," he growled. "I like it. I'd like to fuck it even more."

She smiled, looking like a cat, all feral and cool and distant. "Sorry, big guy, but it's your turn to get fucked today." Then she relaxed her thighs and dropped down on him, letting her weight impale her on him, her cunt opening hungrily to suck him in.

Shea threw back her head and cried out at the thick penetration, loving the way he filled her to the point of blackness, and she hadn't even taken all of him. Intent on doing just that, she braced her hands on his hipbones and pushed, forcing the whole of his cock into her, and then she began to move. There was no gentle roll of her hips, no slow seduction. She simply braced herself and began to ride the hell out of him, fucking him in a pounding rhythm that had him shaking and swearing and arching beneath her, his eyes holding hers the entire time.

He didn't try to take control, not yet anyway, but his big hands found her breasts, fingers gripping her nipples, twisting and pulling until she could feel each little manipulation in the core of her pussy, sucking him like a clamp.

"You are so fucking sexy," he groaned, the rough sound rumbling up from his chest. One hand left her breast to dip between her legs, wetting his fingers with her cream, and then he lifted his fingers to her mouth, rubbing her juices into her lips. Before he could pull away, she gripped them in her teeth, sucking his fingers to the same rhythm with which she was riding his cock.

It was too much. Before she could fight him, he had his hands gripping her hips, pinning her to him as he rolled their bodies. She stared up at him in outrage, clearly not liking having her show overrun, but he just pulled her to the edge of the mattress, planted his feet on the floor, and rammed into her hard enough to jerk a startled cry from her throat.

His eyes were wild and full of emotion, confusing her with their desires when she knew he needed nothing more from her than this. The only thing he wanted was fucking, when she'd wanted to give him everything.

But why was he staring down at her, his beautiful blue eyes liquid and bright, suddenly looking as if he wanted so much more?

He pulled out, then crammed it all back in, every beautiful inch of that brutal cock that was quickly hammering her into submission. She panicked and closed her eyes, breaking the connection.

"Open your eyes." The words were guttural and raw, as if torn from his throat.

She screwed them tighter, but his next thrust plowed so deep, it was as if he hit a switch inside her head, as if the head of his cock nudged against the back of her lids, and they popped open against her will. Ryan snared her gaze and this time, she couldn't look away. She was trapped, and the bastard knew it, because he gave her a slow smile, his lips pulling back over his teeth.

"My turn," he growled.

And he took it for everything it was worth. Whatever detachment she'd tried to use when on top, proving to herself and to him that she could settle for just fucking—at least for now—he shattered beneath the pounding strokes of his cock into her cunt. While one hand secured her hips, his other fisted in her hair, and then his mouth was devouring hers, his tongue teaching her all about possession and hunger and the things that could be found between them if only she'd open herself up and let him all the way in.

He'd breached her body, but now he wanted into her heart, all the way to her soul. She felt the need pour through his kiss—felt it pumping through his cock and in the desperate grip of his hands on her body. It broke her and she went flying over, dragging him with her. They writhed and groaned and broke together, drenching the other in cum, sealing their bodies together in physical ecstasy.

Knowing she couldn't breathe beneath him, Ryan rolled to his side, ready to pull her into him, secure against him, but she scrambled off the bed, backing out of reach as his eyes followed her with a dark expression that was quickly turning from satisfied to furious.

He watched her quickly rummage up her discarded clothes, her fingers shaking as she slipped them back over her sex-flushed skin still rosy and wet with their sweat and fluids, wondering what the fuck was wrong with her. He could feel her pulling away, drawing into herself, and he hated it. And he wasn't about to put up with it, not when he knew with every cell in his body that he wanted this woman for the rest of his life. Wanted to own and love and belong to her forever.

The second her jeans cleared her hips, he sat up on the edge of the bed and asked what in his opinion was a very sensible question, considering what he really wanted to do was toss her over his shoulder and handcuff her to the bed until he figured out what was going on in that bizarre little head of hers. "Where the fuck are you going?"

With uneasy fascination, she watched a small tic develop in his hard, unshaven jaw. Then he asked it again, his tone low and gravelly. "Where the fuck are you going, Shea?"

Her heart tried to fight its way out of her throat, then sank with a resounding thud back to the churning pit of her stomach. "Home," she mumbled, pulling her hair from the collar of her T-shirt.

"You're just going to fucking walk out on me? Thanks for the screw but now I gotta bail? What the hell's going on?"

"Gee, Ry. I'm surprised you have to ask." She tried to appear casual while looking around, wondering where her shoes had disappeared to. "Isn't this your norm, your usual? Mindless fucking and then you're on your way. Since this is your place, I figure the least I can do is bail so you can get on with your life. *You* didn't invite me here—I invited myself."

He stood up, six-foot-four-inches of beautiful, rippling muscle and bone, every delicious bulge and plane accentuated by the wet, clinging fabric of his rain-drenched clothes. Shea nearly swallowed her tongue as he wrenched his jeans back up over his hips, not even bothering to fasten more than the two bottom buttons. She kept watch on him out the corner of her eye while she spotted one shoe and kept looking for the other.

"So we're just supposed to fuck when we want to fuck and that's it? Nothing more? No promises? No commitments?"

"Uh, yeah." *Your usual.*

Oops. Apparently she hadn't kept as good a distance between them as she should have, because he reached her, grabbing her shoulders in an unbreakable hold before she'd known he was even moving. How in the hell did a guy his size move so friggin' fast?

"Goddamn it, there isn't a fucking normal thing about this! You are *not* my norm or my usual or whatever the hell I used to like and I wouldn't want you to be! And for your information, I want a hell of a lot more from you than this!"

Ryan looked over her now clothed body, shaking his head as if he couldn't actually believe what he was seeing. "And you're just going to walk outta here?" he growled accusingly, giving her a small shake. "You're just going to fucking walk out on me?"

Shea took a sharp breath, wondering why he was so angry when this was the way he'd wanted it. And what was he talking about? Just how much *more* did he want? "Uh, you're the one who's been holding out on me, Ryan. You've never once said anything to make me believe you wanted more than this."

Her whispered words had him looking meaner than hell. "Yeah, well, you haven't exactly been pouring out your heart either, have you?"

"Ohhh, you thickheaded jerk! What do you think I was trying to tell you that first night?" Shea felt her own anger and hurt rising, helping her to stand a little straighter, her mouth trembling into a flat frown. "You didn't want to hear it then! Why in the hell should I have thought you'd want to hear it now?"

Ryan let go of her and moved away, running his fingers through his thick hair in a rough, agitated motion, splattering water over his wide shoulders. "I thought that was just the—you know, the sex talking."

Her look said she wasn't buying it.

"Hell," he added, finally getting around to ripping his wet T-shirt off over his still wet head of hair. "I was in too much of a hurry to get back to you today to even wait for the damn rain to let up. That's how fucking nuts you make me. And you can sure as hell bet that if I'd thought you were serious about what you were saying that night, I would've fucking listened!"

Suddenly her head felt light and her heart began to beat with the rapid rhythm of a hummingbird's wings. Any second now it was going to take flight right through the wall of her chest.

"Why didn't you just ask me?" she whispered in a breathless rush, as if she had to work for her voice. Then her eyes narrowed, pinning him in place. "Why didn't you — why didn't you say something? You've had plenty of time to say something — *anything*, Ryan!"

He still looked pissed, but a bit of the tension seemed to ease from his shoulders. There was the barest hint of color to his stubble-covered cheeks. "Because I didn't…didn't know how to say it, damn it! And I've been too damn busy fucking you to figure it out!"

"Oh," she mumbled awkwardly, finding it amazing that she could still blush after everything they'd done together. Everything she'd just done to him.

Ryan watched her, wanting to pick her up in his arms and carry her back to the bed behind him, lay her across it, and keep her there forever. He knew exactly what he wanted — what he'd wanted all along, from the very beginning, but had been running from out of fear. What he'd wanted from the start, when he'd still been such a dumb-ass, trying to convince himself he wasn't ready yet, that he needed to move slow, needed time.

Needed time like hell, he thought with a low curse. What he needed was her sweet little ass in his bed, in his home, in his life, for the rest of his damn days.

He hadn't trusted himself. Hadn't trusted his ability to handle everything she made him feel. But maybe that was okay. Maybe that's how it was supposed to be. Shea made him feel like a raging, bursting mass of emotion, an uncontrollable force of energy and life. Who the hell could be expected to control that? Maybe the right answer was the simplest of all—to just give himself over to it and hold on tight to her with everything he was and would ever be.

The silence stretched between them, rife with tension. Shifting from foot to foot, Shea finally asked, "Well then, what do you want, Ryan?"

All he had to give her was one word, filled with meaning. "You."

It was the hardest thing she'd ever done not to run to him and throw herself into his arms. She wanted it all, everything about him, but she needed to know that she was more than just a passing diversion, a fun time between the sheets. She needed to know if he felt anything for her, if there was any hope for their future, or if her heart was going be shattered into a million irreparable pieces in the end.

Shea believed she was a strong woman, but this beautiful man was her soft spot. He alone held the power to break her, and though she knew she could survive without him, she was honest enough with herself to know she didn't want to. Didn't even want to try.

And she was smart enough to know that loving Ryan with everything she was didn't make her weak. Soft, yes...even vulnerable, but it didn't make her less of a woman. No—it made her strong—a friggin' Amazon, and she was going to be woman enough to hold him forever. "If you ever fucked around on me, I'd make you the sorriest bastard alive. I don't share, not even once. I'm not like all those other women you've known, Ry. What's mine, stays mine."

His mouth twisted as if he'd smile, and then he sobered. "Yeah, well, I wouldn't want you to. I like the thought of you holding on to me as tight and strong as I'll be holding on to you. I plan on being a fucking pit bull where you're concerned."

Her head tilted to the side, big eyes studying him to the point where he felt the uncomfortable, childish need to squirm. "But you said it was just fucking."

"That was just my dumb-ass pride and fear talking, baby. It was a lie," he explained in a low voice, moving closer to her. "What we have is so much more than that, Shea."

"More how?" she asked, her eyes so mesmerizing, he thought he could get lost in them.

"What we've done has been the rawest, hardest, most incredible sex I've ever had," he told her with a small smile, "but it's more than that too. It's...hell...it's—"

As Ryan struggled for the right words, he turned his back on her. His posture remained rigid while he breathed in a jagged rhythm, as if at war with himself over what he'd say.

Finally, he walked to the window and leaned his forehead against the cool glass to stare sightlessly out at the rain-soaked gray of the sky. He didn't see the fat black clouds ready to break open again and unleash their fury, didn't see the gusts of wind that whipped the leaves to and fro, ripping them from their branches.

All he saw was Shea, as if her image had been burned into the back of his eyes. Open or closed, she was always there, just as she'd been since that first time he'd seen her. The only difference now was that he knew exactly how incredible it felt to hold her in his arms, to sink into her sweet little body, to sleep cradled against her womb, their bodies sealed against one another throughout the long night.

For the first time in his life, Ryan knew exactly what he wanted. "What we've, uh, done, it's—" He faltered again and cleared his throat, choking on emotion. He felt terrified and stupid and somehow like the luckiest bastard alive all at once. What if she told him to get lost? Why was he having such a hell of a time getting what was in his heart out in the open? And what if what Hannah had said was right and Shea loved him too?

Oh, God, he prayed. *Please, please let her be right.*

"It's making love, Shea. It may be rough and raunchy, but there's a hell of a lot more underneath it. I love you, damn it!" he said in a coarse, gruff rush, all but growling the declaration. "God knows I tried not to, but—"

Her voice came fast and small, like a whisper of sound. "Why?"

When he turned to face her, she thought he looked like he either wanted to put his fist through the wall or shoot something. "Fuck, Shea. Just look at us," he groaned, his beautiful voice achingly rough. "You deserve a hell of a lot better than me."

Shea shook her head in frustration. *Stupid, stupid, stupid man.* "All I've ever wanted was you, Ryan. How can you not be the best thing that's ever happened to me?"

"You deserve someone worthy, damn it. I've seen and done things that would make you sick, Shea, and you all but fucking glow with innocence. You're too damn sweet for your own good."

She smiled at that. That soft, secretive smile that always made him rock-hard, imagining what she was thinking about. "Do you really love me?" she asked carefully, almost afraid of what he'd say.

Ryan's hands clenched and unclenched at his sides, as if for the first time in his life he didn't know what to do with them. It was an amazing feeling to know she'd rattled him, this brave, gorgeous man who was more of a hero than any of her ancient gods and goddesses could've ever dreamed of being.

"God knows I do," he rasped. "I feel like I'm dying when I'm not with you, like I can't fucking breathe without you next to me." His breath expelled on a harsh sigh, because he couldn't believe what he was about to admit. "It's scary as hell, Shea."

She contemplated him through eyes that were suddenly wiser, older than her years, daring him to reach for everything he'd ever wanted. "Then why don't you just take what you want, Ry?"

"Look, I've never told anyone this," he said quietly, looking lost for a moment. Then he shook it off and shoved his hands into the back pockets of his jeans. "Hell, not Derek, not even Hannah knows all of it, even though she knew me at the time. But there was—uh, this woman."

Suddenly Shea wasn't certain she wanted to hear this. "Ryan, you don't have to explain—"

"Just listen, okay. She was my fiancée. We were going to get married right outta college. She was a few years older than me. Miss Nashville and all that crap. I thought I was a real stud, bagging someone like her, and then I found out she'd been sleeping behind my back with just about every guy I knew."

Ryan rolled his head across his shoulders, trying to relieve some of the tension he always felt when he thought about it, but then he realized the blow to his pride no longer bothered him the way it always had before. Loving Shea made all of that crap seem so insignificant compared to what they had together. Still, she deserved to know all of it.

"Anyway, she slept around with all of them. Shit— friends, enemies, you name it and she'd nailed 'em. When I found out, I got so pissed I went and tracked a group of them down. Ended up being this rich-ass bunch of frat boys, but I was too far gone to worry that they outnumbered me five to one. Anyway, there was a fight and I ended up putting a few of them in the, ah, hospital— and damn near got my ATF application denied. Would have ended up in some serious shit, if my superior hadn't taken it upon himself to investigate the case and present my side of things. After that, I didn't want to have anything to do with another woman, other than to, you know—to, ah, screw her."

"I guess I can understand that," Shea replied softly, her heart aching for him, knowing how hard a man like Ryan would've taken such a betrayal. "I mean, if you really loved her."

"Damn it, Shea, I didn't love her. I know that now. I was angry, furious, but I wasn't heartbroken. I just didn't want to ever go through all that crap again. And then I met you. Hell, I saw you, and suddenly all I could think about was getting you underneath me and keeping you there forever."

One moment he was in front of the window, and in the next he stood before her, cradling her tear-stained face in his strong hands. She hadn't even realized she was crying until his calloused thumbs brushed against the moisture on her cheeks. "You—hell, I don't know how to explain it. You just did something to me. Broke something in me open and I can't put it back together. I don't even want to try. I just want you, Shea. Everything about you. I want it all."

"But what about all those other women?" she asked shakily. "And don't tell me what you think I want to hear, Ryan. I need to know the truth."

His scowl was fierce. "Jesus, Shea. Why in the hell would I want another woman when I've got you?"

She pressed her lips together and shook her head, fighting to hold in the happiness she could feel bubbling up from within. "Just answer the question, McCall."

"No, I won't ever want anyone but you," he told her solemnly. "I'll never so much as look at another woman for the rest of my life. You have my word and my heart on that, baby." His lips twisted, smile wry, blue eyes eating her alive. "Christ, it's all I can do to keep up with *you*."

Her palms covered the backs of his hands, holding him to her. "I love you, Ryan. I want to spend the rest of my life trying to make you happy, make you smile and laugh and—"

"I want you to marry me," he whispered in a gruff voice. It was thick with love, urgent with need. His strong arms wrapped around her, crushing her to his bare chest, while his face nuzzled into the soft, scented skin beneath her ear. "Tell me now, Shea. Please, before I die here. *Tell me you'll marry me.*"

"You want to get married?" Her dazed voice came out in a croak, as if she truly couldn't believe he'd ever want such a thing. She sounded like she'd never even considered it.

Ryan pulled back enough to see her face, his blue eyes glittering with intent. "Damn straight I want to get married. As in you and me together for the rest of our lives. That's what being in love means. That's what forever means, damn it!"

And she could see that he meant it. Every heart-melting, soul-scorching word. Her answering smile was radiant, full of love and the piercingly sweet promise of their future. "Oh, God, yes! Of course I'll marry you!"

"*Damn,*" he groaned against her mouth, trying to kiss her smiling lips, desperate for the taste and texture of her. "You almost had me worried there for a minute."

"Shut up," she laughed tearfully, smacking him on his solid shoulder, so happy she thought she might die. "You already knew my answer, you dolt. As if I'd say no to you."

"I'm not taking any chances." His arms squeezed around her, holding her in case she decided to make a run for it. "We'll go get the blood tests this week. Then go to the courthouse next Saturday with Derek and Hannah."

"Oh, wow." Her voice was soft, the look in her big eyes even softer, melting him. "You seem almost desperate. I'd never even thought you'd want to marry me."

Ryan's hand trembled as he smoothed the silky curls snared in her tears, tucking them behind her ear. "Shea, if you'd said no, I'd have dragged you to an altar and had Derek hold my gun at your back. Desperate? Damn, woman, you have no idea how desperate you make me feel."

This time her smile was impish and dangerously wanton. It was that of a fairy nymph luring him to her lair, but Ryan was going eagerly with a smile on his face. "Hmm, maybe you should, ah, show me."

"Yeah," he whispered against her soft, seductive mouth, thinking of all the ways he'd spend the rest of his life doing just that. "I think maybe I should."

And when he did, she discovered that being fucked by the man of your dreams while he tells you he loves you is one of the best damn things in the world. God, did it get any sweeter than that? Then her climax hit her, pouring through her body with a rush of love and happiness and trust that filled up all those empty hollows, making her bigger…stronger…*everything*—and she knew that it did.

Epilogue
Six months later

Ryan lay in the early Saturday morning sunlight, reluctant to leave the bed and his wife's warm, sleeping body that was wrapped around him. God, he loved sleeping with her. Hell, he loved everything about her.

Without a doubt, the past six months had been the best of his life, and now his future held the sweetest promise of having Shea by his side forever.

Their small wedding ceremony had been perfect, with Shea looking beyond beautiful in a white sundress that made her golden skin glow, her hair flowing past her shoulders in a tumble of silky black waves. Derek had served as best man and Hannah as maid of honor, and afterwards they'd all enjoyed an extravagant wedding brunch at Morton's in Buckhead.

Then Ryan had surprised Shea with a trip to the airport and a short flight down to Key West, where they'd celebrated their honeymoon. They spent the entire time in bed making wild, passionate love. Except, of course, for those times when he dressed her in that sinful blue bikini and pulled her out to the ocean. There he took her in the crystal blue water with the sun beating down on their skin, their bodies rivaling its heat, loving the hell out of each other.

When they came back home, she'd found another surprise when they walked through the door of his apartment. The week before they left had been too frantic with wedding plans to begin moving her stuff into his place, which had the larger floor plan, so they'd alternated nights between the two apartments. While they were gone, though, Derek and Hannah had gone ahead, with Ryan's okay, and moved everything for them as a special wedding present.

According to Derek, Hannah had a hard time keeping her hands off him while they'd worked together. According to Hannah, Derek was living in *lala*-land. Now, six months later, the tension between those two was getting so thick you could all but choke on it, and personally, Ryan thought it was only a matter of time before they found themselves tumbling as hard as he and Shea had.

And, oh man, what a fall. He was so fucking happy his face was starting to hurt from smiling all the time like an idiot, and he knew it was just going to keep getting better and better. This weekend he had another surprise for Shea — they were going house hunting. He'd already contacted a realtor to start looking for properties, and at the top of Ryan's priority list was a pool. Some things were just a necessity, and seeing his beautiful little wife in that damn bikini on a regular basis was one of them.

Shea snuggled deeper into his side, her slim thigh moving over his rampant morning erection, and it was with hot anticipation that he rolled over to properly wake the love of his life.

Of course, his mischievous wife had a plan of her own.

With a sensual grace that had become second nature to her, Shea shifted to her knees, quickly scooting out of his reach until she sat with her back against the polished footboard.

Ryan's eyes narrowed. "Come back here."

"Not yet," she murmured, slowly spreading her legs, revealing the glistening pink flesh of her pussy to his blisteringly hot gaze. "I want to show you something first."

His golden lashes lowered and he smiled with wicked anticipation, loving it when she decided to be a tease and drive him out of his mind. But then, he loved everything about her, and thanked God that she was his every single day of his life. "What happened to my blushing beauty?"

"Oh, she's still here, but you're teaching her fast."

"I can see that," he rasped, watching her movements with dark blue eyes growing darker by the moment. His eyes always mirrored his need, going dark as sin, to a rich midnight blue, when he wanted to fuck her, which was pretty much every minute of every hour of every day.

Shea licked her pink lips, using her fingers to open the even pinker lips of her sex, keeping them spread with one hand while the fingers of the other fluttered over her slit, spreading the sweet moisture already spilling from her body. "Is it a problem for you?"

Ryan growled a dark, dangerous, delicious sound as his muscles flexed and his cock hardened to the point of pain. "No, not a problem," he rumbled. His sexy lips lifted in a wicked grin and he clutched at his chest, "But it just might kill my heart." Then his hand moved down to cup his heavy sacs, "Not to mention my balls."

"Hmm…I guess I better go easy on you, then," she laughed huskily, her fingers dipping deeper, the pleasure of having his eyes on her washing through her system in a blaze of heat, the tiny licks of flame flickering across the surface of her skin.

"You better be careful, Shea, or those sweet lips are gonna be stuffed full of cock before you know what hit you." His gaze stayed on her teasing fingers, the lines of his face growing tight with restraint. "And I don't mean the ones you're talking with." The smile shifted into a playfully lopsided grin—but his expression revealed only hunger and lust. "Are you ready to have that hot little cunt fucked, sugar?"

Her white teeth flashed as she pushed in two slender fingers, rolling her hips as her pussy swallowed them, feeling how tight and wet she was, loving the thought of how she must feel when wrapped around his massive, beautiful cock. "As long as it's by you, Mr. McCall, I'm ready to be fucked every way there is."

"Always—always by me," he grunted, unable to tear his eyes away from her open, glistening, perfect cunt. "No other cock is ever getting anywhere near that sweet, pretty little pussy. You understand that, don't you?" His blue eyes pierced her soul as he stared into the smoky gray of her smoldering gaze. "You do know that I'd kill anyone for touching you, don't you, Shea?"

She nodded, her breath coming faster now, fingers stroking over her clit, loving the way he watched her with so much hunger, so much insatiable, greedy need. Not wanting to wait any longer, she pointed at him. "I'd like that cock in me right now, hard and fast and deep, if you don't mind."

His muscles bulged and his big, beautiful body shuddered from head to toe, making her wonder if he'd come right then, just jerking like a hot stream into the air between them.

"You know," he rasped, dragging her beneath him so that she lay on one hip, her leg held high against his shoulder, completely at the mercy of his throbbing cock. And at the moment, it didn't look as if it had any mercy left. "Underneath it all, you're just plain damn insatiable. Aren't you, sweetheart?"

"And what are you?" she moaned, curling her hot little fingers around him, drawing him to her, delighted when the brutal length of his thick erection jumped in her grip.

"Yours." He bent and kissed her softly, the tender touch of his lips completely at odds with the savage, pleasure-sharp way he intended to take her body. Then the kiss hardened, signaling his intent, and her heavy eyes shot wide in breathless anticipation.

"I'm going fuck you now, beautiful—and when you come," he gritted through his teeth, his deep voice hard with that rough edge of command that always made her melt, "I want you screaming my name. You got that, sugar?"

His fierce expression dared her to disagree. "I always do, Ry. Always."

He stared down at her, beautiful lips parted as his breathing grew heavy, the air around them thickening with unspent desire. Shea rubbed the huge head of his cock between her cream-covered lips, feeling him jerk hard in her grasp, his eyes blazing, going wild with excitement.

"I am so fucking in love with you," he growled, thrusting hard, cramming his cock in with one ramming blow that packed her full—filling her to her limit. She arched beneath him, a raw cry tumbling from her lips, and then she was coming. That quickly—with just that one delicious drive. The orgasm exploded in a blinding rush—

like death—forced out by his sweet, sexy words and mind-shattering penetration.

Ryan rode her hard, just as he'd promised, taking her to that intoxicating point just shy of pain, and her body throbbed in one consuming pulse of ecstasy. He'd wanted her screaming his name, and she did. Four times, to be exact, before he finally lost control and exploded into her hot, sopping cunt so hard he could feel his body pumping from his temples all the way down to the soles of his feet.

Forty minutes later they emerged from the shower together, their bodies buzzing in the sweet aftermath of dizzying pleasure. Shea smiled that delicious smile of hers as she watched him towel off his gorgeous body, and he wanted her all over again as he watched her do the same.

Christ, she was going to be the death of him, because he was never going to get enough of this woman.

Then she got another surprise, one he'd been looking forward to all night long—even more than the carnal fuck-fest they'd just gorged themselves on.

When she opened the medicine cabinet to take out her birth control pills, the pack was empty. Odd, when Shea knew she'd still had at least two weeks worth of little pink tablets left to take.

"Oh, man," she said with a confused frown, "this is so weird. I could've sworn I was only in the middle of this pack."

Ryan was careful to keep his expression perfectly neutral while he ran the towel over his hair. "Yeah, you were."

She blinked up at him, a small smile beginning to curve the edges of her kiss-swollen mouth. Her heart began beating double-time. "I *was*," she said slowly, "but, um, now I'm not?"

He still hadn't changed expression, but his blue eyes were sparkling with devilish delight. "That's about right."

Shea narrowed her eyes. "And would you by chance have anything to do with this bizarre occurrence, Agent McCall?"

Ryan grinned, cocky and self-sure as he pulled her to him, wrapping his heavily muscled arms around her, trapping her with their strength. "That I would, Mrs. McCall."

Shea was laughing when he lowered his head to kiss her, his lips warm and delicious. The kiss went on for long, drugging minutes, and then he said against her mouth, "I love you, Shea. I want to be with you forever, for always, baby. I want to make an army of pretty little girls like you and little bullies like me to share the rest of our lives with. Whadya say, beautiful?"

"Hmm," she sighed, her heart and life full of a love more meaningful than she could've ever hoped for. "You really are a cocky bastard, but I say that's about the best idea I've ever heard."

Ryan laughed a deep, dark sound full of wicked intent. He nudged his stunning erection into her soft belly, eager for the time when it would be swollen with his child, and asked, "Wanna start now?"

With a naughty giggle, Shea whipped his towel from around his waist and licked her lush lips while eyeing her husband's most enthusiastic body part. "I think we already have," she teased in a husky rasp, kissing a hot trail down his hard stomach. Then lower, to where he was even harder.

When her moist, delicious mouth closed over the broad, blunt tip of his cock, sucking him deep, right down her throat, Ryan threw back his head and groaned with sweet, savage satisfaction. *Oh man, oh man, oh man.*

Then Shea did one of the things she did best, and brought the gorgeous stud to his knees all over again.

Enjoy this excerpt from:
A SHOT OF MAGIC
MAGICK MEN

© Copyright Rhyannon Byrd 2004

All Rights Reserved, Ellora's Cave Publishing, Inc.

At six-five, he was tall and mean and muscle-honed from all the long, grueling hours he spent training other *Magicks* – Warlocks and Witches – in the arts of combat and self-defense. He had thick, reddish brown hair that he normally kept trimmed much shorter than his outrageous cousins, light green eyes, and golden skin. He was well dressed, always in control of his strong, passionate emotions, and wealthy enough to afford any luxury he wanted, from houses to cars to women. Though sex was one thing he'd never had to pay for.

He'd always had a look of danger, but now that look took on a more sinister character. His hair was longer, shaggy around the strong bones of his face, jaw dark with auburn stubble, big body wrapped up in ragged jeans, a black T-shirt, and big black boots as he left his house to pace the early, fog-filled streets of Edinburgh.

He looked like the kind of man you wouldn't want to meet in a dark alley, and he felt like one as well. And to be honest, he didn't know how much more of this he could take.

You'll take as much as you have to, man, his Warrior's pride warned. *Because you canna let those blasted fools win. Not this time! You've pledged them your bloody loyalty, but they havenna any claim on your cock!*

Yeah, well, too bad the governing High Council of Magicks — made up of his five outrageous uncles — thought otherwise.

They'd put a bloody curse on him, the well-meaning fools. One that changed his women into fucking animals every time he shot his blasted load. And the only way around it was to find his *bith-bhuan gra* — his soul mate.

His uncles, it seemed, had taken it upon themselves to ensure that he stopped sowing wild oats and began planting a few instead.

In the belly of the right woman, of course.

It was intolerable. He was so full of sexual frustration his skin felt like it was about to burst. Hot, tight, and disturbingly prickly, like an itch beneath the surface that remained just beyond his reach. He'd tried alleviating the painful pressure on his balls himself, taking matters into his own big hands, but ended up putting his fist through his shower wall when he'd been unable to bring release.

That was apparently yet another one of the Council's twisted concoctions. According to their sadistic curse, he could only achieve an orgasm with a woman. And if he didn't want to find himself shooting his cursed load of magic in front of another friggin' furry pet, he had to find the true woman — whatever the hell that meant.

He'd found *her* three weeks ago, when he was on a walk just like this one. And he'd dreamed of her each night since.

There was only one problem.

Well, one on top of the fact that his uncles had plagued him with a freaking curse on his cock and he couldn't screw without shooting a load of magic that turned his women into angry animals, leaving them craving a piece of his ass to chew on.

His balls were blue, his time was running out, and instead of searching for the true *Cailleach*—his *bith-bhuan gra*—he'd become obsessed with *her*. She was goddamn fascinating, beautiful and intelligent and spirited as hell. So different from any woman he'd ever known before.

There was just that one minor, somewhat unfortunate detail.

The woman who haunted his sleep and every waking hour was not a *Magick*.

She was not of his kind.

No, the woman of his dreams was a fucking mortal.

About the author:

Rhyannon Byrd is the wife of a Brit, mother of two amazing children, and maid to a precocious beagle named Misha. A longtime fan of romance, she finally felt at home when she read her first Romantica novel. Her love of this spicy, ever-changing genre has become an unquenchable passion—the hotter they are, the better she enjoys them!

Writing for Ellora's Cave is a dream come true for Rhyannon. Now her days (and let's face it, most nights) are spent giving life to the stories and characters running wild in her head. Whether she's writing contemporaries, paranormals…or even futuristics, there's always sure to be a strong Alpha hero featured as well as a fascinating woman to capture his heart, keeping all that wicked wildness for her own!

Rhyannon also welcomes mail from readers. You can write to her c/o Ellora's Cave Publishing at 1337 Commerce Drive, Suite 13, Stow OH 44224.

Also by Rhyannon Byrd

Why an electronic book?

We live in the Information Age—an exciting time in the history of human civilization in which technology rules supreme and continues to progress in leaps and bounds every minute of every hour of every day. For a multitude of reasons, more and more avid literary fans are opting to purchase e-books instead of paperbacks. The question to those not yet initiated to the world of electronic reading is simply: *why?*

1. *Price.* An electronic title at Ellora's Cave Publishing runs anywhere from 40-75% less than the cover price of the <u>exact same title</u> in paperback format. Why? Cold mathematics. It is less expensive to publish an e-book than it is to publish a paperback, so the savings are passed along to the consumer.

2. *Space.* Running out of room to house your paperback books? That is one worry you will never have with electronic novels. For a low one-time cost, you can purchase a handheld computer designed specifically for e-reading purposes. Many e-readers are larger than the average handheld, giving you plenty of screen room. Better yet, hundreds of titles can be stored within your new library—a single microchip. (Please note that Ellora's Cave does not endorse any specific brands. You can check our website at www.ellorascave.com for customer recommendations we make available to new consumers.)

3. *Mobility.* Because your new library now consists of only a microchip, your entire cache of books can be taken with you wherever you go.

4. *Personal preferences are accounted for.* Are the words you are currently reading too small? Too large? Too...**ANNOYING**? Paperback books cannot be modified according to personal preferences, but e-books can.

5. *Innovation.* The way you read a book is not the only advancement the Information Age has gifted the literary community with. There is also the factor of what you can read. Ellora's Cave Publishing will be introducing a new line of interactive titles that are available in e-book format only.

6. *Instant gratification.* Is it the middle of the night and all the bookstores are closed? Are you tired of waiting days—sometimes weeks—for online and offline bookstores to ship the novels you bought? Ellora's Cave Publishing sells instantaneous downloads 24 hours a day, 7 days a week, 365 days a year. Our e-book delivery system is 100% automated, meaning your order is filled as soon as you pay for it.

Those are a few of the top reasons why electronic novels are displacing paperbacks for many an avid reader. As always, Ellora's Cave Publishing welcomes your questions and comments. We invite you to email us at service@ellorascave.com or write to us directly at: 1337 Commerce Drive, Suite 13, Stow OH 44224.

Discover for yourself why readers can't get enough of the multiple award-winning publisher Ellora's Cave. Whether you prefer e-books or paperbacks, be sure to visit EC on the web at www.ellorascave.com for an erotic reading experience that will leave you breathless.

WWW.ELLORASCAVE.COM